As he remembered the moment when he'd almost kissed Suzi, Mitch muttered to himself, "What was I *thinking*?

"She 's my friend," he reminded himself. "I couldn't even *think* of her in that way."

Suddenly he realized that was a lie, because he *had* been thinking of her in that very way. When he held her tonight, he'd held a desirable woman, a beautiful woman, an earthy woman, one who was strong yet vulnerable, determined yet childlike in some ways, soft and yielding yet able to stand on her own two feet.

He stared at his reflection in the mirror. "Well, it ends here. Tonight. Just because I've decided to get married doesn't mean I need to go around looking at *every* woman like that."

It was a long time before he found the solace of sleep. And when it finally came, his dreams were haunted with pictures of a dark-haired, dark-eyed angel named Suzi....

Books by Cheryl Wolverton

Love Inspired

CHERYL WOLVERTON

married in Lawton, Oklahoma, at age nineteen, and had her first child, Christina, eleven months later. And three years after that, Jeremiah was born. Giving up college, she happily settled into motherhood, wanting to spend her time with her children. It was during this time that she discovered that she enjoyed writing. Being the pack rat of the family, she actually found stories that she had written in grade school.

After seventeen years of marriage, Cheryl says her best friend is still her husband, Steve. That's one of the reasons why she loves to write romance novels. They're about friendships, love and the ups and downs of life. They show that there really is still a chance at happy endings. After nine books, two children, her own ups and downs and seventeen-plus years of marriage, she still believes this.

Cheryl has been a finalist in many prestigious contests, including: the Romance Writers of America RITA Award, the Holt Medallion and *Romantic Times Magazine*'s Reviewer's Choice Award. Watch for Cheryl's upcoming books.

For Love of Mitch
Cheryl Wolverton

Love Inspired®

Published by Steeple Hill Books™

STEEPLE HILL BOOKS

Steeple Hill™

ISBN 0-373-87111-2

FOR LOVE OF MITCH

Visit us at www.steeplehill.com

Printed in U.S.A.

A friend loves at all times…

—Proverbs 17:17

To the keeper of my heart. You've been there for me always, in the hard times, the devastating times and the good times. When things were blue, when things were dark, when things looked bleak, you were a beacon lifting me up above that. When in pain or sickness you never once complained but were the steady companion and friend I needed. To my best friend—Steve— husband and holder of my heart. I love you.

To Christina, Jeremiah and Chris (my nephew) who is currently living with us and is learning just what a writer's life is like.

And to my dear friend and critique partner, Cherri Munoz. Pam Schlutt, my publicist: Thank you so much, dear woman, for the load of work you have lifted from my shoulders so I could finish this book!

Chapter One

"There's the woman I should marry."

Mitch McCade leaned back against the counter of Hill Creek's only diner and observed Leah Thomas as she hurried across the street toward the local general store. Her blond hair blew up around her tiny delicate face. He watched her brush it back before looking one way and then another, smiling at old man Joe who sat in a chair out in front of the white storefront before passing through the door.

"You should what?" Suzi Fletcher's voice resounded with shock.

Mitch glanced over his shoulder at her as she walked around the counter.

She removed her apron and dropped down in a seat next to Mitch. "And who are you talking about?"

Mitch watched Suzi absently remove the pins from her black hair and rub her head. She winced and her dark brown eyes revealed her exhaustion. "I said, I've decided to marry. And Leah Thomas is the woman I ought to snag."

Suzi stared at him in disbelief for a heartbeat and then burst out laughing.

Mitch scowled.

Only Suzi would laugh at Hill Creek's sheriff. Most treated him with respect and courtesy, but not Suzi. They'd grown up and gone to school together and had been friends their entire lives.

"You're kidding, right Mitch?" She giggled again and said in Spanish, *"Ella es muy bonita, pero—"*

Mitch shook his head. "Are you done here? I'll walk you home."

Suzi's smile left. "You're serious about this, aren't you, Mitch?"

Mitch stood and slipped his beige cowboy hat onto his head. His khaki pants and shirt, the Sheriff's uniform of Hill Creek, Texas, accentuated his tanned skin. He shifted before stretching his wide shoulders. "Yes, Suzi, I am."

Suzi caught him off guard when she walked up and rested a soft hand on his arm. "Oh, Mitch. Tell me this isn't about settling down and having a family."

That's what he got for telling all his secrets to this woman, Mitch thought, disgruntled. "You know I want kids, Suzi. I want to give them something I never had growing up."

"Parents."

He simply shrugged. They had been over this many times.

"Your parents died in a sky-diving accident, Mitch. Your brother Zach did his best."

Mitch walked to the door of the diner and held it open for Suzi, waiting for her to leave. "It's not the same as having parents. And I want to find a woman who'll make a good mother and want to settle down. I want to give them what I didn't get,'' he said, using the words that had become a litany as of late—since watching both of his brothers become newlyweds.

Suzi walked out of the diner, her white uniform glowing in the setting sun. Turning, she locked the front door, pocketed the keys and then started down the sidewalk toward home. ''There's more to marriage than kids. What about love? Commitment? What if she doesn't want kids?''

Mitch's footsteps echoed quietly on the sidewalk as he and his lifelong best friend walked down the street toward the edge of town where Suzi lived. ''Leah's a school teacher, Suzi-q. Of course she wants kids. And she's a widow—at least, that's what has been said. I imagine she likes marriage. As for love...''

Mitch shifted away from Suzi a bit. ''Love between a man and a woman will come eventually. It's not a prerequisite for marriage.''

''Mitch McCade!'' Suzi whirled on him, as he knew she would. ''I ought to box your ears for that. You know better. Just look at Zach and Laura or even Julian and Susan.''

Mitch scowled. He wasn't surprised that she'd bring them up. Still, he refused to believe that the happiness his brothers had found would come his way. ''Those are my brothers. This is me. I just don't know if I'm capable of that type of love, Suzi. I mean, what is love, really? Some falling-down emotion? Sorry, I don't believe that. Commitment? Makes more sense to me.''

Her features immediately softened. ''Oh, Mitch.'' Briefly she hugged him. Mitch didn't mind. Over the years they'd shared a lot of hugs. Pulling her into an embrace, he took the petite woman in his arms and held her close, feeling the tiny body that had become so familiar to him as her slender arms wrapped around him. He absorbed the warmth, dropping his chin to the top of her head and sighing wearily.

''Why can't you just forget your past and realize what a good and loving person you are?''

Her soft voice drifted up to him, all of her concern, her worry, and her caring enveloping him in an uneasy feeling of guilt. Especially since he wasn't the only one with ghosts in his past.

"Like you've done yourself?" Mitch asked quietly.

Immediately his best friend stepped back, her arms falling to her sides. Her gaze went blank as it always did when he mentioned her past. He wanted to shake her. He and Suzi had shared everything—except one important thing.

"Mommy!" A dark-haired little girl came running out of a tiny, rundown house, and headed straight for Suzi.

"Hello, chica." Suzi lifted her five-year-old daughter into her arms.

With a loud groan of pleasure, she tightly hugged the little girl, simply enjoying the tiny arms encircling her neck. She knew Mitch watched her.

She had never shared who had fathered her child and deserted her, leaving her alone with a child to raise.

He didn't whisper and point and speculate like the others. When he asked, it was out of concern and worry for her. But she just couldn't tell him who the father was, or why that one night, she'd defied her beliefs, her God and everything she had been raised to believe.

Oh, Father, she thought, *I know it's under the blood, but consequences, they never end, do they?*

"Guess what, Mommy? Miss Thomas let us draw today. We got to draw anything we wanted. I drewed a picture of Heaven."

Suzi set her daughter down and nodded to the babysitter as she left. "Did you bring it home? Do I get to see?" Suzi asked.

"I'll get it."

They watched Kristina run back toward the house.

"Where does she get that energy?" Suzi murmured.

"That's a child for you," Mitch replied, walking over and sitting down on one of the iron chairs that needed a good sandblasting and painting. He dropped his hat on the small metal table next to the chair. Suzi smiled, thinking how many times Mitch had sat right there and they'd talked. His golden skin glowed in the descending sun, his features sharp from shadows. She could still see the stubble from a long day that touched his square jaw.

"It was a scorcher today. The diner felt like an oven," Suzi said. "That breeze feels so good." Dropping her head back she closed her eyes and worked on relaxing. Concentrating on his jaw wasn't something she wanted to do right now. It would lead to places she didn't want to go. Which reminded her... "So, tell me, Mitch, how do you propose to catch Leah Thomas and make her Leah McCade?"

Suzi kept her eyes closed, trying to ignore the pain that question caused. Old pain, half healed, but still there.

"Well, now..." Mitch drawled which drew her eyes reluctantly open and to him. She couldn't resist the boyish little I-have-a-plan drawl.

But his eyes. His eyes were what confirmed it. She knew that look. "Oh, no you don't, Mitch. I am not getting involved in this. Don't you dare ask me."

Mitch attempted a wounded puppy-dog look. "But you're my best friend, Suzi-q.

What are friends for, if not to help out each other in a time of need?''

She scowled at him.

Mitch chuckled. "Come on, honey. You'll like it. It'll be fun."

She stuck her nose in the air before turning her back on him to look elsewhere. Every time she saw that look she eventually caved. She wasn't going to cave this time. She was going to be a strong pillar. "I will not. I can guarantee you that, Mitch McCade," she muttered quietly, definitely certain she would not want to participate in anything that involved helping him find a wife.

Kristina ran back out with a picture in her hand and crawled up into her mother's lap. Suzi paused in her mutterings. "Ooh, this is beautiful, honey. You did a wonderful job." She kissed Kristina on the head. "Can I hang it on the living room wall?"

Kristina giggled. "You already got too many. There won't be enough room."

Suzi cupped her daughter's cheek. "We'll make room. Now, give me a kiss and then go play for a bit. Mommy is talking with Uncle Mitch."

Suzi accepted the wet kisses from her daughter and then watched as she ran off to swing on the tire in the front yard.

"She's growing like a weed," Mitch said softly.

Suzi nodded. "Yes, she is. So fast."

It seemed like only yesterday that Suzi had passed out in school. Could it have been that long since they'd rushed her to the hospital and she'd gotten the news of her condition? She was suddenly pregnant, alone and a high-school dropout. And with few exceptions, she was shunned by the community. Of course, the father of her child had made sure of this with a few well-placed rumors.

Suzi thought bitterly of how alone she'd been during the pregnancy and birth. Even her mother turned her back, refusing to forgive her. Suzi had withdrawn, talking to no one, associating with no one, until her daughter was a month old and her mother had died of a sudden heart attack.

Seventeen and suddenly on her own, it

had been a nightmare that had turned her back to God. "You left for college just before she was born," Suzi said now to Mitch.

Mitch sighed and nodded. "I should have waited. After all, I never finished. However..." He looked over at Suzi and grinned.

"Uh-oh, here it comes."

Mitch shook his head slowly as he said, "Not at all. Actually, I'm taking college courses through the mail. I have to go take tests every so often, but I haven't told anyone. In a few more months I'll have a degree in criminal justice."

"Oh, Mitch!" Stunned, Suzi could only stare. "You didn't tell me!" Regaining her composure, she offered a smile. "I'm so happy for you. Why didn't you tell me before now?"

He grinned sheepishly, reminding her how insecure he was in many ways. She should have known that something this important he wouldn't share immediately.

"I wasn't sure I was going to finish."

She watched that engaging grin of his

spread across his face and his eyes turn all dark and coaxing. "Anyway, I think the best way to get to know Miss Leah Thomas is through the class she teaches at school. And since you work at the school in the mornings until noon, I've decided you can help me."

She stared. "We're back to that again?" Knowing the scowl wouldn't work this time, she tried reasoning with him. "I'm only a part-time assistant, Mitch. That won't help you."

"Yes, it will. You're the one who assists with the schedules of the extracurricular activities. Why not schedule me on safety classes? After all, we've been having problems with some of the kids in town lately. And I do teach those drug-awareness classes each year."

Suzi shook her head. Leave it to Mitch to have found a way to spend time with the woman he had set his sights on. "It wouldn't also have something to do with the fact that I also volunteer a lot for Leah since she's my daughter's teacher?"

Mitch flashed that killer grin at her.

"How'd you guess? So, Suzi-q? Will you help me?"

"I swear, Mitch," Suzi muttered. "Why you can't see when someone cares for you and go after them instead of someone who most probably has an aversion to police officers—"

"Someone as in who, Suzi?" Mitch asked, surprise clearly evident on his features.

Suzi realized what she'd said and nearly clapped a hand over her mouth in horror. She couldn't believe she'd blurted that out. She was tired, more tired than she'd been in a long time. Because of that, she'd let that bit of information slip right out into the open. "Someone who? I don't know. I just meant that Leah doesn't seem to like police officers—any of them, and here you are talking about wanting to marry her. At least, she acts like she doesn't like police officers. Seems she had problems with some in the past or some—"

Mitch waved a hand. "Forget her for a moment. Go back to the other. Who is it, Suzi? Who have you been talking to?" he asked, grinning engagingly, trying to coax it out of her.

Suzi scowled, knowing how he was when he got a hold of something. "No one," she reiterated.

"Aw, come on, Suzi-q, tell. We don't keep secrets."

"That voice isn't going to work, Mitch McCade. So stop it right now." Getting up, she started toward the house.

She heard him follow.

"Okay. I'll just have to find out on my own."

Suzi glanced over her shoulder and snorted. "There is no way you'll find out. You're like all other men, brain dead and blind."

Mitch tsked and followed her over to where she started watering the flowerbeds. The springtime heat had wilted the white daisies. "Now, now, Suzi, that's not very nice. You know how I am when I decide to find out something. I think maybe I should just to prove to you I can."

Turning the water from the daisies to the

lilies, Suzi sighed. "But I thought your goal was to marry by the Fourth of July party?"

"I can find out who it is and still marry by the fourth of July party." He shrugged.

Suzi paused, the hose in her hand. Turning she gazed up at him, her brows going up in disbelief. "In two months? You honestly think you can find this woman, court her, woo her, convince her to marry you and then plan a wedding in two months? I don't think so."

"Is that a challenge?" Mitch goaded, his eyes gleaming at her unintentional dare.

Suzi glared at him, wondering how she'd gotten herself into this mess. "No, it is not." She raised the hose as an implied threat of what would happen if he continued along this line of thought, but he simply ignored it.

"If I don't win, I'll paint your house, free of charge."

Suzi paused and studied him. Her house could really use a good painting. It was in awful shape.

There was no way he could win, but that wouldn't be fair to him.

"You won't win," she said, and sounded so sure it gave Mitch a moment's pause.

Then he grinned. "You won't know unless you take the challenge."

"What do *you* want out of this?" she asked suspiciously. She would get her house painted. She thought that would be ideal for him to do when he lost. She and Mitch were always making these types of bets, and she loved it when he lost.

"If I lose, which I won't," he said cockily, "you'll have to do my laundry for a month." His lips curled up with disgust. "I hate laundry."

Suzi laughed. "I know that."

Mitch relaxed, feeling his face spread into a small half smile, echoing the feeling within him. He liked to see Suzi laugh. She so rarely did. "It's a bet then," he said.

"I didn't say I agreed."

"Aw come on, Suzi. We used to do this all the time. What are you going to lose? It's just someone who's interested in me. That's all."

She glanced over to where her daughter was playing and then back to Mitch, her dark brown eyes glittering with hidden emotions. "Okay. Why not? I need my house painted."

She grinned, and he wondered why she looked so confident. Of course, he knew that when Suzi wanted to keep a secret, she was the world's best at keeping it.

"I'm not making a mistake with this, Mitch McCade. After all, you know I'm good with secrets. What could possibly go wrong?" With a quirky little smile she headed off to gather her daughter and go in for dinner, her confidence high.

"I'm not sure, but with you, Suzi, we always seem to find trouble."

Grinning, he slowly followed her.

Chapter Two

Had Suzi really thought everything would go smoothly with Mitch McCade doing the challenging?

She was plumb crazy. That's all it was. Crazy, insane, utterly out of her mind to put up with this. She'd thought it would take him a few days to get started.

No....

She'd gotten a call last night from Melody Carter and during the conversation she mentioned Mitch had called her to chat. To chat! Melody had been totally flustered. The librarian of the town, Melody kept to herself and was very quiet. She had few friends, went to few socials. She just loved to read. Poor Melody was certain she'd done something awful and the sheriff was trying to find out about it—though she couldn't imagine what it was she'd done.

Suzi reassured Melody that Mitch was probably only trying to get to know most of his constituents better, especially after all that had happened in Hill Creek when a drug ring had been busted. After she'd hung up, Suzi decided she'd have to talk to Mitch about scaring poor Melody.

This morning, however, before Suzi had had a chance to call him, Sharon Barker, the postmistress, had paused in the school office to remind her that the school's box fee was due and mentioned that Mitch had stopped at her table in the café for breakfast. He'd asked how her job was going and went on and on with nonessential chat before finally getting up and leaving. Sharon had been so surprised at how kind and neighborly Mitch had appeared that she had actually been late opening up the post office—the first time in over four years.

Shaking her head, Suzi had assured her

Mitch was always friendly and then wished her a good day.

Mitch was out to win.

Suzi wasn't going to allow that.

She had decided to set to work on an alternate plan. The problem was, she hadn't come up with anything yet.

Perhaps she could distract Mitch with the rumors she'd heard that many members of a gang had moved over into Steel Hill County and were reopening their drug ring.

But Mitch wasn't the sheriff there.

Then there was the idea that she could possibly interest him in starting an after-school program for the boys. They had kicked the idea around at their school for quite some time—find someone to teach the kids basketball and start up a team. But would that really distract him?

She didn't think it would take up enough hours. What was she going to do? Leaning over to dig in the files to her left, Suzi pondered that problem right up until flowers appeared before her face. "Oh!"

Jerking back in surprise, Suzi let her gaze follow the arm up—to find Mitch standing there grinning from ear to ear. Looking at the flowers, she realized Mitch was in rare form, ready to conquer the world—which meant bad news for her. "Good morning, Sheriff. How can I help you today?"

"These are for you."

"Oh?" she asked, arching an eyebrow and staring at him. Very slowly and deliberately she crossed her arms in front of her. "I hear you've been harassing the local women, Sheriff."

"Me?" Shaking his head, he grinned. "Not at all. After all, it is my sworn duty to protect." Waving the flowers, he said, "Come on, Suzi. I'd hate to have to give these to Laura. You know, Zach just might get jealous."

Suzi rolled her eyes and snorted. "You are impossible," she said, exasperation in her voice, though her features told a different story. He could be playful and fun-loving when he was around her, but Mitch rarely let down his guard with others. She was certain it was because at one time, before he'd gotten right with God, he'd been considered the bad boy in town. Who would have guessed him to end up the sheriff? And he knew she couldn't resist that look of his—or the daisies.

Before she realized his intent, he reached out and lifted her hand into his. Stroking her fingers, he smiled gently. "So, lovely lady," he drawled, his voice warming her. Suzi's breath shorted in surprise.

"Mitch?" she questioned. He had never done this before.

"Does the woman who is interested in me work here?"

It took a moment for his words to register. "Mitch McCade!" she gasped, and jerked her hand back.

He hooted with laughter before taking his seat. "Put those flowers in water before they die," he directed. "You're looking better than you did last night."

Shaking her head, she picked up the flowers and moved to get her vase from the counter. Pouring some of her drinking water into the container, she said absently, "I rested better last night. Kristina actually slept the entire night."

Mitch frowned. "She sure hasn't been sleeping well lately."

"I know. Your sister-in-law thinks it's a bug going around. If it doesn't get better she said to bring her by the clinic and they'd run some tests. I think she's well now, though." She arranged the flowers and then placed the vase on her desk.

"Good. We don't want the little angel sick."

Suzi chuckled at Mitch's nickname for her daughter. "So, why are you really here today?"

A smile curved Mitch's lips. "I'm going to teach some classes against drugs. And guess who the principal said I could start with?"

Suzi sighed. "Leah's class?"

Mitch nodded.

"You really like her, don't you?"

Mitch shrugged. "She's everything I want in a woman."

Suzi wondered if that were true. He wanted a woman to give him children, both of them to be the parents he had wanted his own parents to be. Still, since Julian had married, Mitch had been restless, roaming the streets, unhappy, looking for more. Marriage was what he had decided was missing from his life.

Suzi was afraid it was more than that. Suzi was afraid what he was searching for was the love both of his brothers had found. First Laura, who'd come to Zach with amnesia from an accident. Then Julian with Susan "Freckles" Learner who had come to town to be his partner at the clinic outside of town. Suzi thought Mitch saw that love and wanted it, but just didn't recognize it as more than marriage.

"Come on. I'll take you down to her class. It's about time for the kids to get back from recess."

"So, Suzi-q, you gonna come to church with us, Sunday?"

Suzi sighed. "I wouldn't be welcomed."

"You won't know until you try."

"You're never going to let up on me, are you?"

Mitch stopped her in the hall simply by turning and stepping in front of her. Reaching out, he took her hand. "What type of friend would I be if I didn't worry about you, honey?''

Suzi dropped her gaze, feeling tears. "Mitch—"

"You don't have to say anything, sweetheart. I've been in the same place as you were. I know what it feels like to think the entire town is against you and hates you. That's just a lie from the enemy. Sure, there are some sticks-in-the-mud out there who can't see past the beam in their eye, they're so worried about your splinter, but not all of them are bad. Why don't you join the family on Sunday, Suzi? You know Laura would sure love you there. She's taken quite a liking to that daughter of yours. And Susan could sure use a few friends. Heaven knows, she's scared enough away after the rumors that she broke Julian's arm.''

"She did break his arm," Suzi replied dryly, lifting her gaze to smile at Mitch.

"My type of gal," he teased, shaking his head, the disbelief in his eyes. "It's still hard to believe. It was an accident, though. She swears she was only trying to hug him when he told her he loved her. Those two—"

A grin kicked up the corners of his mouth as he said, "What do you say? You sit by me? I'll wear my uniform. No one will say a word."

"If I sit with you what will Leah think?"

Mitch cupped Suzi's chin and held her gaze. "You're my best friend, Suzi. You have been for years, since grade school, since my parents' death. No one will ever replace that. Okay?"

"But if you marry…"

Mitch shook his head. "You'll always be my Suzi. How could I give you up as a friend? Honey, you're like the sister I never had."

When she winced, he frowned. "You okay?"

"Just fine," she whispered. "Let's go see Leah."

He slipped an arm around Suzi and gave her a squeeze. "You're a good girl, Suzi. I'm going to come by your house Sunday whether you like it or not. I want you to come to church with me."

Suzi ignored him, though inwardly it pleased her he cared so much. Instead, she walked into the kindergarten class where Leah Thomas stood writing on the chalkboard. Her pink, drop waist dress and white T-shirt made her look half her age. Soft blond hair danced around her angelic face.

Everyone loved Leah.

No one knew anything about her, though. Leah didn't let anyone close.

Hearing them, Leah turned. A warm smile spread across her face. "Suzi, hi. What are you doing here?"

Her soft voice echoed with musical warmth, until she saw Mitch. Her glow faded a bit, and she clasped her hands, though she did try to keep the smile. Still, it was very obvious Leah was uncomfortable. "Hello, Sheriff."

"This is Mitch McCade, Leah. I don't think you've met him. He's the one who has been doing the drug classes this last year."

"I heard about that awful incident out at the clinic. They found a huge stash of drugs, didn't they?"

"From drug runners who were trafficking through here before, that my deputy and sister-in-law discovered."

Leah nodded. "And you're here to talk to my class today?"

Suzi watched the way he turned on the charm, smiling so gallantly. "Yes, ma'am. Can you squeeze me in when the kids get back?"

Leah hesitated, then nodded. "Of course, Sheriff."

It was obvious to Suzi that the woman was totally impervious to Mitch's charm. Glancing at Mitch, she thought that he might be wondering why Leah seemed so distant, too. Had they met before? People rarely were so wary unless they had a good reason. Shaking her head, Suzi said, "I'll let you get back to work. I'll be in the office if you need anything."

Turning, Suzi hurried down the hall, leaving Mitch in the room with Leah Thomas.

"Suzi?" Mitch called out.

Suzi paused and turned. He stood at the

door, a grin on his face. "Sunday morning, don't forget."

"Men," she muttered and headed back to her office.

done a silly thing like... Sunday morning, don't forget."

"Okay," she mumbled and flicked back to her side.

Chapter Three

"Men," Suzi muttered squirming on the pew.

"What was that?" Mitch asked from her left, glancing down at Suzi.

She elbowed him to make more room.

"Mommy. Uncle Zach is gonna let me sit in his lap."

The giggle from the right drew her gaze to meet Zach's grin.

Suzi rolled her eyes.

"Told you you'd have support," Mitch said smugly from her left.

A tap on her shoulder from behind had

her twisting around. "Just ignore them," Dr. Susan McCade said.

"Hey, Sis," came from in front of Suzi—a whole row of kids sitting with Susan's oldest brother, Chaseon. They must also be related to Dr. Susan.

Susan answered, "Yeah?"

As Chaseon answered, Suzi stared up to Mitch. "Do you know," Suzi whispered, "Because you have surrounded me with a battalion of soldier-ready saints of God, every single person in here is staring."

Mitch nodded. "That was the idea, honey. You have the entire McCade clan as well as the Learner family, our in-laws, supporting you. Even Laura's brother, Mark is here."

Suzi finally laughed. "I can't believe you people," she whispered.

"That's my, girl. Laugh."

"Um, not to point this out, but Leah just walked in."

Mitch looked around and sure enough, there was Leah strolling down the aisle. She glanced at him and nodded before hurrying on down to an empty pew. Mitch frowned.

"There is something too odd about her reaction. I've never met the woman, and yet she acts like she is scared of me."

Suzi reached over and patted his leg. "Please, Mitch, give it time."

Slowly Mitch shook his head. "This isn't about chasing after her, Suzi. That woman fears me, I think. And I'm wondering why."

"Let's all give thanks to The Lord for His love endures forever!"

Suzi glanced at the young song leader who called that out. With a smile at the congregation, he asked them to stand and then lifted his hands in prayer and praise. Suzi felt a wave of warmth and joy spread through the church as they began to sing.

Slowly, bit by bit, she relaxed as the peace of God descended. She noted her daughter really enjoyed the service, clapping and singing. It surprised Suzi that no one called the little girl down since she was a bit more exuberant than the others in the church.

When she saw the warm looks from different people in the service, Suzi stared, stunned. She continued to watch them and noted that some she had been certain hated her and her daughter didn't act that way at all. Slowly the shock faded and relief flooded her—relief and such a breaking of the pain she had held in her heart. True, there were many that still snubbed her, but was Mitch right? She'd been so busy hiding, and yet, here were these people accepting her. Shaking her head, she realized she was crying. Tears flowed, as she thought about the five long years she'd hidden away in fear of rejection, but no one here was rejecting her at all.

She felt an arm slip around her and with surprise saw that it was Mitch's brother, Zach. He squeezed her gently and before she comprehended what she was doing, she turned into his chest and began to cry. Slowly, all the pain of the past surfaced and rushed from her heart as renewal took place. The bitterness of rejection, fear of more rejection and loneliness all fled. Suzi vaguely heard Zach and Laura praying with her as she cried.

Strangely enough, after trying for so long

to hide away, it seemed perfectly normal that when she did break down, it was in church. Finally her tears slowed and she pulled away, embarrassed.

Mitch was waiting. Leaning down, he whispered, "Welcome home, Suzi-q."

That was all that was said. When the singing ended, they seated themselves.

"This is the day The Lord has made. I will rejoice and be glad in it," the pastor said, as he walked up to the pulpit. "Behold, all things are passed away. All things are made new." Grinning, the pastor winked at the audience. "I think we've seen things made new today, during this song service. Open your bibles and today we're going to discuss letting go of the past. Starting anew, today, living today as the first day of the rest of your life. For, do you know that's how God sees you when you come to Him and seek forgiveness? He wipes the past clean and starts anew."

Suzi glanced suspiciously at Mitch. He lifted his shoulders in a shrug. "I didn't say a word, Suzi-q. Honest. Someone's just been spying on you, I'd say," he joked in a whisper.

Suzi felt so good she didn't argue. She knew Mitch would never betray her. Looking down, she became absorbed in reading the Word with Mitch as the pastor read out loud.

Then he preached.

And the service was over.

Suzi hadn't felt this alive, this good since her entire world had come crashing down around her six years ago. When the pastor dismissed them, Suzi turned to get Kristina but found her sound asleep on Zach's shoulder.

"You are coming to dinner, aren't you? Then Kristina can have a riding lesson," said Laura.

Suzi hesitated. "I really don't want to intrude on your Sunday dinner."

Laura pulled herself up and rubbed her large belly. "No, please. I'd love the company. Zach won't let me do a thing. My boss—" Laura scowled at Mitch "—has me on part-time *desk* duty when he lets me come in at all. And my doctors insist I rest.'' She cast a look at Julian and Susan and observed. ''You'd be a breath of fresh air in the stale ranch house of bondage.''

Suzi couldn't help but chuckle. ''Very well, Señora,'' she said softly. ''I'd be honored.''

''You really should come out to visit us more often. Kristina loves the horses. And with all of Freckles' gang living out there now,'' she said, referring to Susan by her nickname, ''there are always kids around.''

''I appreciate the offer,'' Suzi said, smiling warmly at Laura.

''We'll meet you out there, Sis'' Mitch said to his sister-in-law. Then turning his attention to Suzi, he asked, ''You want to go by your house and get anything before we head out there?''

''Yes. If you don't mind.''

''Is it okay if we take Kristina with us?'' Zach asked.

Suzi smiled. ''She'd love that.''

''See you out there then.''

Zach slipped an arm around his wife's

very pregnant body and escorted her out of church, Kristina asleep on his shoulder.

She turned back to Mitch. "Okay?"

"I'm at your beck and call."

She smiled at the way he said that.

He leaned down. "How about Penelope Harrington?"

"Hmm?" she asked, confused.

"It's her, isn't it?" He pointed to the very bookish-looking young woman currently staring their way.

Suzi turned, met her gaze and the woman's nose went in the air before she strolled away. Hurt, Suzi flinched. "No. It's not her."

Mitch's hand slid around her waist. "Good. She'll never catch anyone with an attitude like that."

"It's okay, Mitch."

"No, it's not. But we can't change everyone's attitude. Come on, honey."

He escorted her down the aisle toward the exit. Suzi was about to breathe a sigh of relief at escaping any more confrontations when the back door swung open and she came face-to-face with a person she had never expected to see again.

She came face-to-face with her child's father.

Chapter Four

There were gasps as people recognized who had just entered the church. Mitch stiffened next to her. Everyone stared.

Mitch was the first to speak. "Hello, Noble. I thought you were in jail."

Suzi simply stared. He had been convicted on drug charges and sent away. She'd thought she'd never see him again. She had finally relaxed. He was gone. He couldn't cause any more problems. After so many long years of fear and agony that he would reveal her secret, that he would finally tell everything that had happened, she had thought to live again in peace. And had.

Until now.

Noble Masterson was back.

And with him, the secret she had kept so carefully.

Noble glanced from his hated enemy—a McCade—to Suzi, his gaze running over her, then back to Mitch. ''The sentence was overturned. Seems the judge didn't agree with you or the jury that I was guilty. Tsk, tsk, Mitch. Law-abiding citizens getting falsely arrested.''

Mitch started to say something, but Suzi tightened her hand on his arm. Arguing with Noble would only cause problems. And she had to get out of there. No telling what he might say. Oh, why had he come back now?

''Noble?'' Bate Masterson, pale as a ghost, came hurrying from the front of the church toward his son.

''Hello, Father,'' Noble called out cheerfully.

Suzi was going to be sick. Without waiting for Mitch she pushed past the group and went outside. Blindly she crossed the yard and found a tree near the parking lot to lean against. She concentrated on taking deep breaths, working to calm herself.

"Are you okay, Suzi?" The soft voice of Leah came to her, and Suzi realized she wasn't alone.

Suzi glanced up and found Leah standing there, in her pale blue dress, worry creasing her brow. "I'm fine. I just...it was too warm in there," Suzi answered.

"Oh. Yes. It does get awfully hot here in the springtime doesn't it? Do you want me to get you some water?"

"Suzi, are you okay?" Mitch came striding up.

Leah shifted uneasily. "I'll let the sheriff see to you," she said to Suzi, and with a small nod hurried off.

Baffled, Mitch watched Leah, before turning his gaze back to Suzi. "You look a bit green."

Suzi watched to see if there was a sign that Noble had said anything to Mitch. He stared blankly at her. Had Noble announced something like that in the church, Mitch certainly wouldn't be so quiet. Relieved, she relaxed. "I'm better. It was just a bit too hot."

"Let's get you in the air-conditioned truck. We can go by your house, you can change, pick up what you need and then we'll head for the ranch. Okay?"

Suzi nodded. "Perfect," she said low, only wanting to get away.

And that's just what they did. After stopping by her house, they were on their way out of Hill Creek headed for Zach's nearby ranch.

"Tell me, Suzi," Mitch said now, as they drove along the road to Zach's house which, at one time, had been the family house. "What did you think about church today, other than it was too hot?"

Mitch casually observed Suzi as he drove. She was beautiful today. She'd changed into jeans and a button-down top. Her ponytail accentuated the curves of her face. Devoid of makeup, her natural beauty shone through brightly.

At his question, he noted her features softened. "It's been hard, Mitch. I hadn't realized what I'd been missing." A soft sigh escaped her lips. "I suppose sometimes we get so caught up in our own problems that we can't see that we're hurting ourselves by hiding."

Then her features darkened.

"Suzi?" he queried, encouraging her to continue.

"I wish I could talk about it all, Mitch. I just don't know if…"

She glanced out the window. Mitch followed her gaze to the barren plains, the rolling prairie grass dotted with red dirt and occasional boulders. Cacti dotted the fields and barbed wire with posts lined the highway. What did she see out there? Mitch wondered. He had a feeling it mirrored what was in her eyes—emptiness. "What, honey? What don't you know?" he asked gruffly.

"If I'll ever completely get over the past."

His hands tightened on the wheel in frustration. Suzi had made one mistake and though he knew God had forgiven her, he also knew Suzi hadn't forgiven herself. It was so troublesome. Suzi was closer to him than most of the people in town. She knew all of his secrets, his hurts. She had been there for him numerous times—so why couldn't he take the hurt and pain away for her that he saw darkened the sunlight from her eyes?

Taking a deep breath, he decided to change the subject instead of dwell on something that hurt his friend.

"I was out here the other day when Zach was giving Kristina her riding lesson." Mitch turned the four-by-four onto a dirt road and headed down the long, unpaved trail toward the ranch house.

"Kristina mentioned that. She thinks you're pretty cool."

Mitch chuckled. "And I think she's pretty cool, too. She impressed me with how much her riding skills have developed. She has a natural talent. Poise is what Laura called it."

Mitch relaxed, relief sweeping through him, as Suzi's frown dropped away and a soft smile as sweet as a summer morning drifted into its place. "Poise. She wants to take ballet. Did I tell you that?"

Mitch groaned. "Why do all the girls want to take ballet?" he muttered.

The last of the haunted darkness fled as Suzi's eyes regained the gentle twinkling that so reminded Mitch of a girl intent on mischief.

"Poise," she finally said, then burst out laughing.

Mitch grinned. "Looks like I'll have to tell the gal she already has poise and perhaps she should take self-defense instead. She's growing up to be quite a beauty. Probably need those lessons when she hits high school."

Suzi shook her head. "I imagine before she gets much older one of you McCades will teach her how to handle herself. I swear, Mitch, you, Zach and Julian are such mother hens at times."

"Hey!"

"Roosters?" she asked innocently.

"Don't remind me of that," he muttered.

Suzi giggled. "I'll still never forget you losing that stupid rooster in the schoolhouse."

Remembering the incident, a reluctant

grin kicked up the corners of Mitch's mouth. "You must admit it sure stirred up things. I'll never forget having to explain that to Zach, though. And how angry Noble's dad was. I don't think Noble has ever forgiven me for that." He shook his head as he pulled up to the house and parked the four-by-four.

Jumping out, he came around and pulled the door open and reached into the back seat to get his own saddle and change of clothes he'd had stowed there.

Suzi clambered out.

"Mommy!"

Mitch grinned as he watched Kristina, dark hair bouncing, limbs flying, run straight for her mom and leap at her.

Suzi caught her. "Hello, baby. Have you ridden yet?"

"No-o-o," the little girl drawled out in an exasperated voice that reminded Mitch too much of Freckles Learner. He smothered a grin as Kristina continued, "Aunt Laura says we have to eat first."

"As you should," Suzi said, and then gave her daughter a resounding kiss on the head. Lowering her to the ground, she turned her, patted her bottom while giving her a nudge toward the house. "Go wash up. We'll be right in."

Kristina raced off toward the house. Suzi stared after her, that pain he'd seen earlier creeping back into her features. Mitch said nothing, but moved up next to Suzi in silent support.

Finally, without looking his way, Suzi whispered, "I don't want her hurt, Mitch. I can't talk about it because I don't want her hurt."

A tender ache surrounded Mitch's heart. "No problem, Suzi-q. Know I'm here though, if you need me."

Turning, Mitch headed off toward the barn.

"My brother giving you a hard time?"

Suzi's glance darted toward the voice. She hadn't heard Zach come out the front door and down the steps. She wondered just how much he'd heard. "You know better than that," she murmured as Zach McCade, head of the house, stopped next to her. With his dark good looks, Zach, the eldest

McCade at thirty-seven, was a very handsome man—very handsome but very unavailable.

"I beg to differ there, Suzi. How many times have I broken you two up when you were beating up on Mitch for something he'd done?"

Color touched her cheeks. "That was years ago, Zach."

"Yeah, it was. I don't know of any fights lately, now that you mention it, though Mitch does tend to keep to himself."

Suzi harrumphed. "Not lately he hasn't."

"Oh?" Zach asked.

Realizing her best friend would hit the roof if she told Zach before Mitch had a chance, she simply cocked her head and smiled at him. "Ask your brother."

Eyeing her curiously, Zach slowly nodded. "When it concerns the both of you in on a conspiracy, believe me, little one, I will."

"Little one? Zach, I have a five-year-old child. Will you stop calling me that!" She shook her head at him and then turned, striding into the house amid the laughter that followed.

"He knows how to get to you, huh?" Laura said, walking slowly into the living room. "That man isn't happy unless he's poking the bear, so to speak."

Suzi smiled at Laura. "I've known him long enough to know I should ignore him. Here, sit down, let me finish. You don't need to be on your feet this close to delivery."

Suzi took Laura's arm and helped her to the couch. "Same thing Susan Lear— McCade said." She smiled ruefully at Suzi. "My sister-in-law."

"Too many McCades popping up to keep track of all of you," Suzi acknowledged.

"Suzi, I think you and I need to have a talk."

The squeak of the screen door and the deep tones of Mitch's voice ran right down Suzi's spine, both causing goosebumps but for different reasons.

"Uh-oh," Laura muttered, and rolled her eyes. "The boss is mad." She gave Suzi one of her deputy-sheriff-in-hiding looks as she politely sank down onto the couch.

"You won't hear an argument from me there," Suzi said grinning. "I also think he's upset."

Laura chuckled on cue.

Turning, Suzi faced Mitch. "Yes?"

"What did you tell Zach? Woman, don't you know he won't let me hear the end of it now that he realizes I'm getting married?"

"You're getting married?" Laura gasped and jumped to her feet.

"Married!" Zach said, shock evident in his voice.

"Married?" Julian asked, he and his wife, Susan "Freckles" McCade, coming out of the kitchen with dinner. "Who's getting married?"

"Our brother, evidently," Zach said.

"Really?" Freckles beamed. "Congratulations!"

"To whom?" Julian asked, curiosity lifting his brows high.

"You didn't tell him?" Mitch demanded, shock and exasperation in his tone.

Suzi grinned innocently, lifting her shoulders in an it-wasn't-my-fault shrug. "Not a word."

Turning, Mitch gave his brother a dark look. "Dirty trick, big bro!"

Suzi moved over by Laura and eased her back onto the couch. Laura frowned at Suzi, then at her doctor and sister-in-law, Freckles McCade, who called out, "Stay."

"I'm not a dog," Laura muttered.

"Who are you marrying?" Dr. Julian McCade, the youngest of the McCades demanded of Mitch, ignoring all the banter around them.

Mitch's chin shot out mulishly and his gaze turned downright black. He didn't answer.

"Keeping a secret?" Zach asked, then strolled past Mitch to ease down by Laura. He lay a possessive hand on her tummy, stroking it and sending a tender look his wife's way.

"Well?" Julian asked. Kristina, coming down the hall, saw Julian and ran over, grabbing him around the legs for a quick hug before going to Laura and imitating Zach's actions by stroking Laura's tummy.

Suzi watched Mitch. His gaze hadn't left her once he realized his mistake. He was still sizing her up; trying to figure out just how he'd been set up and what part Suzi had in it. She could only smile mischievously at him. "You know how your family is, Mitch. It would have come out eventually. How many women have you called now?"

"What?" Zach's gaze lifted to them in genuine confusion.

Mitch finally sighed. The look he gave Suzi promised retribution. Oh, not that they'd have a knock-down-drag-out fight like when they were younger. No, Mitch was grown. He had other ways of making her pay. She grinned at him.

He shook his head at her, then motioned toward the table. "Come on, let's eat. I'll tell you over dinner. But right now, I'm starving."

Suzi gave him a look of support and he shrugged in response.

"Good enough for me," Laura said and stood, breaking the silence.

Obviously, Freckles felt the same way for she chimed in. "Amen."

They all made their way to the table and sat down together. Zach asked the blessing, and then napkins hit laps and bowls started around the table.

"So, brother, what have you gotten into this time?" Zach asked mildly as he spooned some mashed potatoes onto his plate.

Mitch passed the corn to Suzi who sat on his left. Glancing to Laura on his right, Mitch scowled.

"Don't scowl at me. He was your brother before he became my husband." Turning her head, Laura smiled softly at Zach.

"Yeah, but you've only encouraged his curiosity."

"Now, Mitch," Suzi said. "From what I remember, he's always been like this." She spooned food onto Kristina's plate. Her daughter had tuned out the adults' conversation as she concentrated on drinking her tea.

Mitch sighed. "Very well. It's simple." A slow smile curved his lips and his gaze went to Suzi.

Oh, dear. She knew that look. He was out for mischief now, and his family was the one in for the shock.

"I've decided to marry by July 4th, thanks to Suzi. She told me there's someone in town here madly in love with me, and I plan to find out who it is and then settle down in marriage."

"I did *not* say that, Mitch McCade!" Suzi protested loudly. She should have known he'd pull her into this. "I told you your scheme to chase after a certain someone was crazy when there were..." she said, her voice fading. Then muttered, "Okay, but I didn't say it *that* way."

Mitch grinned. "So, there you see, Zach. I'm planning on finding that woman and settling down."

Zach stared at Mitch, then his gaze went to Suzi. Suzi noted how deeply Zach stared at her, making her want to shift uncomfortably. She knew, however, that shifting would surely tip Zach off.

Then he smiled, tenderness briefly showing in his eyes before he turned and said to his brother. "Well, then, Mitch. I hope you finally find her."

Suzi nearly fell out of her chair. He knew. She was certain of it. He knew! But, how could he know?

"And then I hope you'll inform us," Julian said from the opposite end of the table, breaking into Suzi's frantic thoughts. Freckles, who sat across from Kristina and next to Zach, nodded her agreement.

"Weddings can be wonderful."

It was obvious from the glow in Freckles' eyes that she loved Julian deeply. Suzi hadn't seen Susan aka Freckles take her gaze off Julian for more than a minute.

"And painful," Julian muttered, which caused everyone to laugh. Suzi remembered Julian's wedding of not even four months ago. They'd come back from the Northeast, with a house full of in-laws, and three weeks later held the wedding. Nearly an entire baseball team of sisters- and brothers-in-law. However, with all that help, they'd gotten the old ranch house cleaned up and livable quickly—despite the fact that Julian, in his hurry to get Freckles off for the honeymoon, had tripped down the stairs and broken his ankle.

It was a family joke now that Julian had spent his honeymoon in a cast.

"Well, you can't blame that on Freckles this time," Zach said now.

"I'll gladly take the blame," Freckles said, and reached out to touch Julian's hand. "It kept him with me, nearly immobile, for six weeks."

Another round of laughter sounded. Slowly it faded, and they all settled down to eat. Suzi smiled as she realized the worst was past. Mitch had finally let his family know what was going on. They weren't upset or overly concerned and, most importantly, they wouldn't hear about anything through gossip. Now she could sit back and rest. His family would watch out for him. She had covered all the basics to make up for her original blunder. Things would get better now. After all, nothing worse could possibly happen. She'd taken care of everything.

Chapter Five

"You've got to be kidding!"

Mitch grinned at Suzi's incredulous expression.

Leaning forward, he rested his arms on the corral fence. "If it's not Laura's sister, then..."

"Are you guys going to ride—or talk all day?" Angela asked, slowing up as her horse reached the corral.

Mitch smiled at his niece. "Back from friends?"

"Daddy said you were going riding. I only came by to pick up some stuff and watch Daddy give Kristina her lesson. Laurie is gonna be out here, too.''

"The entire clan," Suzi murmured.

"That's our cue," Mitch said. Winking at his niece, he said, "Tell your dad I forced Suzi to go riding with me to pry out her deepest secrets."

The gasp from Suzi told him he'd definitely got her dander up.

"Sure, Uncle Mitch." Angela said grinning. "But I bet she gets the best of you in the end. She always does." Smirking cheekily, Angela bounced on into the barn.

Mitch watched her go. "Is that so, Suzi? Do you always get the best of me?"

"Of course." Suzi's voice was low, her mutter definitely laced with exasperation.

Mitch moved over and slipped his arms around her giving her a quick hug. "Don't be upset, Suzi-q. I'm only teasing."

Her body was stiff, unyielding for only a moment, before she relaxed against him. "I know," she mumbled into his chest.

Mitch simply held her, looking over her head out past her at the horses and cattle in the distance. He could hear men down near the workers' quarters as voices would rise with laughter or arguments. It was a beautiful day. The sun was behind the clouds, but it didn't look like it would rain for a few more hours yet. The sky mirrored his mood.

Marriage and children. Would that fill the emptiness he felt so often? He loved God but lately had been restless. For so long he'd kept himself in a shell, afraid to reach out, unwilling to reach out and get burned, to lose someone again. But maybe, just maybe, marriage was the answer. Both of his brothers had found peace. He could see it in their eyes. He wanted that peace, too. Making a family would give him a chance at that peace again—the thing he'd lost when his parents died.

He felt the softness of the woman he held closely now, her warmth. She had saved him in many ways when he'd lost his parents. If she hadn't given him a black eye that day, he might have actually ended up trying what those "friends" had been offering.

"It took me a long time to live down that black eye," he murmured out loud.

Suzi started in his arms, hesitated, then pulled back. Clearing her throat, she turned and headed toward the barn. "What in the world made you think about that now?"

Mitch grinned. "I was thinking how you've always been there for me, Suzi-q. Through thick and thin."

Glancing over her shoulder, she shot him a wary look. "Don't even ask me again who it is."

He chuckled. "Okay, okay. I'll give you a break if you go riding with me."

Suzi nodded and went on into the barn, noting Angela had been and gone, and she hadn't even realized it. Going over to Jingle Bells she proceeded to saddle her. "You sure you want me to go? After all, how often do I get to ride?"

"Not enough. It'll come back. Don't worry."

She grunted as she pulled the cinch tight. Finally she climbed on the horse and not waiting for Mitch, rode out. Mitch only smiled. He finished tightening the cinch on his own horse and then mounted.

"Wait for me!"

Mitch glanced around and found Kristina running toward them, her little legs pumping as she raced. Mitch turned the horse. "What is it, sugar?"

"I wanna ride with *you!*"

Mitch looked toward the porch. Zach stood there, his arm around Laura. Calling out loudly, he asked, "Do you mind? She doesn't want a lesson today."

Mitch leaned down and scooped up Kristina seating her in front of him. After a wave at Zach and Laura, he headed out after Suzi.

It was easy to catch up with her. Jingle Bells was giving her trouble. Grinning, he rode toward Suzi who was sawing on the reins. "Problems?"

"Not...exactly..." She finally managed to get the horse to head in the direction she wanted. "Is this horse always so ornery?"

"Yep. Laura was training her, but since Zach found out she was pregnant, he's put a stop to nearly all of her riding."

"I can see why," she muttered.

Mitch watched as, with sheer determination, she brought the horse under control.

Kristina giggled.

Mitch chuckled and headed out across the field, knowing Suzi would follow. She knew the path as well as he. They'd spent countless hours down by the pond. "So, Kristina, why didn't you want a lesson today?" he asked as they rode.

"'Cause you was going to the swing and I like the swing."

Mitch glanced at Suzi who had caught up with them. "Apple doesn't fall far from the tree." He winked at Suzi.

Suzi shrugged. "Definitely her mama's girl. And I'm glad, Kristina, that you wanted to come." She gave Mitch a superior look.

"Do you think this one—" he nodded at Kristina "—will stop the questions?" he asked mildly.

With a sweet grin, she nodded. "I know she will."

Kicking the sides of her horse Suzi took off.

"Look at mama! She can ride fast," Kristina whispered in near reverence.

"Your mama has been riding a long time," he returned.

"As long as Uncle Zach and Aunt Laurie and you?"

Mitch ran his fingers through the dark hair of the child in front of him. "Oh, yeah. She's ridden for years and years."

Suzi came trotting back grinning. "It's been a long time," she said, breathing hard. "Especially with a horse who has a mind of her own."

Mitch turned his horse to the well-trodden path near a copse of trees. Cutting through, he came out on the other side and right to the pond. "You'll be sore tomorrow riding like that, Suzi."

Dismounting, he reached up and helped Kristina down.

With a squeal, Kristina took off right for the water. "Can I, Mom? Can I?"

Suzi hesitated. Mitch touched her hand. "She'll be fine. We're both here."

Her shoulders relaxed and she nodded. "Go on, honey."

Kristina plopped down and started pulling off socks and shoes.

"I guess I don't get to spend enough time with her and she knows that," Suzi murmured, as she tethered her horse.

"That might be partly true. But she loves you and you love her deeply. She knows that."

With a sigh Suzi stood. "Laura and Zach sure look to be in love. I don't doubt they didn't mind in the least having time alone."

Mitch walked over to the swing. "Have a seat, Suzi."

Lifting an eyebrow, she studied him. He shrugged. Her curious look made him uncomfortable. "You can use the pampering and rest. Let me push you while Kristina tries to catch fish."

He watched her face ease into a grin. Walking over, she sat down. "I still can't believe you told her you can catch a fish with your hands."

Mitch chuckled. He pulled back the swing, then set it into motion. "She has fun trying. Let her enjoy it. Who knows, maybe one day, Suzi-q, she just might catch one."

Suzi relaxed as the swing arced back and forth. Her eyes drifted closed and the sweet scent of wild flowers surrounded her. "Laura has been good for Zach," she murmured. "I don't remember him smiling much before."

Strong, sure hands grabbed the rope and pushed again, sending her forward. "Yeah. He sure has changed since Laura. So has Angie."

She floated forward, the wind pushing her hair back. She heard her daughter call out, "There was one!" Then the frustration was gone as she started trying to coax the fish to come closer.

Mitch chuckled low. His deep voice sounded so peaceful, gentle....

"Do you think much about the rapture, Mitch?" she wondered. Suzi thought about how they all waited for Christ to return any day and snatch them all away. This was a hope Jesus gave and Suzi believed the Scriptures when they said comfort one another with these words.

She floated back for another push of the swing. Hands once again pushed her forward. "Yeah, sometimes. I mean, it'll sure be a lot better one day. And…"

"And you'll see your parents again?" she asked softly.

There was a short moment of silence. "I don't know. I'm not sure. I want to sometimes but others…I just don't know, Suzi."

She nodded, her heart going out to him. She knew he still hurt deeply over the loss. She wondered if the loss of a parent was something you could ever get over.

"What about you, Suzi?"

The quiet question penetrated her thoughts, and she focused on what he'd asked. Slowly, her gaze went to her daughter. "Yeah. I do. One day we'll be gone but…"

"Kristina?"

She nodded again to Mitch. "It's silly. The Bible says things will be so different that we can't even imagine it, but I guess in our tiny minds we can't understand that. I worry about Kristina, about her not knowing who or how…about her birth…and if I go before I have a chance to explain. It's hard, Mitch. I don't know when to tell her things, what to tell her. I don't even know if that's normal or it's just me having these problems."

"I know it's hard, Suzi," Mitch agreed, and Suzi knew he was offering to listen with that statement.

With a deep sigh, she slowed the swing and turned to meet his gaze. "Do you know, she came home the other day telling me that boys and girls are different. Then she explained exactly how. I hadn't even explained that yet."

Mitch grinned. "Now I bet that was an experience."

Suzi shook her head. "You don't know the half of it. I ended up sitting her down and we had a long talk about the differences. She's in kindergarten. I never would have dreamed..."

A chuckled escaped Mitch's lips. "Well, yeah. I understand that. I imagine being a single parent is harder than being one of two parents." His features darkened and Suzi wondered if he thought of his parents. "I know Zach had a hard time. I tried to help with Julian, but he was a stubborn kid.''

"You were as well, Mitch McCade," Suzi replied.

A cool wind blew up whipping her hair into her face. She pushed it back behind her ear. "Now that's not entirely true," Mitch drawled.

"I got it. Look!"

Both turned to Kristina who came running up. For a moment, Suzi thought her daughter had caught a fish. Not at all. In her wet hands she held a smooth stone.

"Whatcha got there, Kristina gal?" Mitch asked kneeling down.

"It's a rock. See how pretty it is? I founded it in the pond."

"Found," Mitch corrected, taking the rock. "It sure is pretty. What are you going to do with it?"

"Take it home and put it with my others. On my shelf."

Suzi rolled her eyes. Mitch met her gaze, smiling. "You sure do have a rock collection. Want me to keep it for you so it won't get lost?''

"Uh-huh," she said, shoving it in his hand and heading back to the water, the conversation over.

"Do you know, she probably has fifty rocks by now."

"Now she has fifty-one," he murmured, and slipped the rock into his pocket.

"You're so good with her, Mitch," Suzi said. Why oh why couldn't he see he had turned out to be a wonderful person? Why did he insist on feeling left out because he didn't have a family?

"I want a family, Suzi," Mitch said and dropped down against the tree. Bending one leg, he crossed his arms at the wrist, resting them on his knee.

"You have a family," she said softly. "Your brothers, sisters-in-law."

"I want kids."

"I know you do." What could she say to him? His heart ached with a void he rarely let others see. She wished she could fill it for him, but as far as he was concerned she was just Suzi-q, best friend. Which brought them back to his crazy scheme. "So, you think you'll really find someone to marry by Independence Day?''

Mitch's dark gaze lightened and he grinned at her. ''Course I do.''

She grinned back, glad to see the darkness gone from his face. ''Good. Now, do me a favor, Mitch.''

''What's that, Suzi?'' he replied.

''Get my daughter and let's head back. We're gonna have rain in an hour or two.''

A loud clap of thunder sounded and Mitch glanced up. ''Uh-oh,'' he said.

Kristina looked up, squealed and headed, full force, across the grassy area right toward them.

''Oh no,'' Suzi groaned. ''Let's get out of here now.''

''Too late,'' he replied. The sky opened up. They watched. A sheet of rain in the distance headed their way.

''I knew I shouldn't have gone riding,'' Suzi muttered darkly.

Mitch chuckled. ''Come on, let's see how long we can stay ahead of it.''

He took off, scooping up Kristina in his arms and racing toward his horse.

Suzi shook her head. Her exasperation faded as she listened to her daughter's shrieks of joy. Taking off after Mitch, she only made it two feet before the rain hit. "Agh!" she cried out.

Mitch shouted, laughing out loud.

Suzi quickly untethered her horse. "I swear to you, Mitch McCade—" she started as she swung her foot into the stirrup "—if I were a betting woman, I'd think you pla-a-a-a"

The saddle slipped, her foot twisted and pain shot through her ankle.

In shock, she let go of her horse. It jumped forward. She went flying. She heard Mitch's shout, but not much else. Pain exploded.

Everything went dark.

Chapter Six

"Suzi-q? Time to wake up, honey."

Suzi heard the faint voice and smiled. In her dream she was lying in bed, married and they had to get up because…

Her smile faded.

She was wet.

"Come on, honey. Kristina is worried."

Kristina?

The dream faded. Suzi was wet, cold and it wasn't a bed she was lying on. Blinking, she opened her eyes. Things around her blurred before slowly coming into focus. A tree was above her and a man next to her. Mitch. And there was Kristina, biting her lip working hard to be brave. Summoning up the best smile she could, Suzi smiled at her daughter. "Ouch."

At her mother's voice, Kristina suddenly flew forward and fell on her mom's chest. "You wouldn't waked up. You fell and we came over and you didn't answer me."

Suzi winced in pain. When Mitch started to reach for Kristina, she waved him off. "It's okay. How long was I out?" she asked of Mitch.

Her entire mind was fuzzy, her head pounding.

"About thirty seconds, a minute at the most. How are you feeling?" Mitch asked, still kneeling there in the rain.

Glancing from him to her daughter who still hugged her, she simply frowned. "How about we get back to the ranch now?"

"Can you ride, Mommy?" Kristina asked worriedly. "I know I felled off my horse the other day and hurt my—" she glanced back at Mitch then back to her mom and whispered "—I fell on my behind and couldn't ride."

Suzi touched her daughter's cheek. "I'm sure I can ride."

"I wouldn't suggest that, Suzi. Not after what happened. Kristina, go hold the reins to your mommy's horse and let me help her up there okay?"

Kristina jumped up and headed toward the horse who stood idly munching a bush.

"She obeys you well," Suzi murmured.

"She's scared," Mitch said bluntly. "Now, let's see just how well you can sit up on your own."

Reaching down, Mitch slid his arm under her shoulders and helped her sit up. Suzi's face went white. "Whoa there, honey."

Gasping, she grabbed his shirtfront. "Man, that hurts," she muttered into his shirt.

"You can't ride, can you?" he asked, though he already knew. There was no way this woman could guide a horse a mile back to the ranch house.

"I think, maybe, well…if you help me…"

Gently Mitch ran a hand over her head.

"You've got a bump the size of an egg back here. We'd better not risk it."

"But how are we going to get back?" she asked.

The uncertainty in her voice shocked Mitch. Never before had he heard her sound like that. Suzi had always been so in control. Even when she was pregnant she'd never once acted as if it bothered her. Suzi was stoically brave. She didn't waver—did she? Cupping her cheek, he tilted her head to look into her pain-filled face.

And then he saw it. In her eyes was uncertainty. He only caught a glance before she covered it by lowering her lashes, but he'd seen it. He swallowed.

Somehow, seeing Suzi so needy disconcerted him. Suzi didn't need anyone. Suzi was Suzi, the woman who was so self-sufficient.

An odd feeling overcame him. "Let me handle this, Suzi," he said. Moving he carefully helped her to sit against a tree.

"I'm not an invalid," she muttered.

"Maybe not, honey, but you're as white as a ghost. You even have pain marks around your mouth. So don't you try telling me you can control that ornery horse on your own."

"I won't," she admitted, low.

That settled it. For Suzi to agree on anything like that meant she was indeed in a lot of pain. "I have an idea. Just a second."

Mitch turned and went over to where Kristina stood. "Hey, sweetie," he said, ruffling her wet hair, "how would you like a lesson on horse riding from Uncle Mitch?"

"You don't give horse lessons," Kristina argued.

"Well that's true," he admitted ruefully to the little girl who stared at him like he had two heads. "However, wouldn't you like to ride back to the ranch house on Thunderbolt all by yourself? You could brag to Uncle Zach."

"Really?" Kristina squealed with delight.

"Well, I'd have to hold the reins, sweetheart, but yeah, just think, an entire mile by yourself."

"Totally cool," the little girl said and immediately went to the other horse.

"Let me adjust the stirrups," he warned, and set words to action. Then with a heft, he seated her on the horse. He checked the stirrups again, and turned to Suzi.

Suzi had pushed herself up and was standing—and looked absolutely awful. Striding over, he swung her up into his arms. "You don't take orders well," he grumbled.

"Have I ever?" she returned, though she collapsed against him.

"No," he replied, lifting her onto the horse. "Hold onto the saddle horn."

He swung up behind her and then repositioned her in front of him. "Is this okay?"

"You can't let Kristina ride by herself," Suzi said weakly.

He heard the worry in her voice and how soft and weepy it sounded. "That's just the mother talking, honey. You know she can sit a horse well. And I'll have the reins."

"I can't believe I did something so stupid. I loosened the cinch just a bit when I tethered Jingle Bells. I completely forgot to tighten it. And my *foot* slipped..."

"Shush, Suzi. God was watching out for you. You're okay. Kristina is okay. And I even think the rain is letting up some."

"Great." Suzi sounded thoroughly exasperated.

"Hey, better late than never. A mile in pouring rain wouldn't be fun."

"We could wait if it's letting up," Suzi said.

"No way," Mitch said. "I'm not allowing you to stay out here with a bump like that. Freckles and Juls would have my hide."

Reaching over, he caught the reins to Kristina's horse and looped a knot in them before slipping his belt and hooking it between the reins and his saddle. "Now you sit still and we'll go. Ready Kristina?" he asked turning to her.

"Yes!" she said.

Mitch had to grin at her restrained exuberance.

They started off at a slow pace. Mitch glanced down at Suzi who lay in his arms in front of him, one hand gripping his thigh in a death grip, the other hand around his back holding onto the saddle behind him. He realized, for the first time, Suzi was a lot smaller and more fragile than he'd noticed before. Had she always been that way? he wondered.

Or maybe it was working two jobs and raising Kristina alone.

How long had she been wearing down before his eyes and he hadn't realized it?

Everyone had a breaking point.

He'd never considered Suzi might have one. For most women, being pregnant and not married would be a strain that would break them in such a small community. Suzi had weathered that fine as far as he could tell.

But lately…

He reached up and pushed her dark hair behind her ear. The curve of her cheekbone revealed her pain in the way her skin tightened over it. "It'll be okay, honey. We'll be home in minutes. Juls or Freckles can have a look and give you a shot for the pain."

"I'll be…fine," she whispered through gritted teeth. "I just feel like an absolute fool."

Mitch grinned. "Well, it isn't the first time for either of us. So let it go."

A painful chuckle escaped her lips. Tipping her head carefully back, she smiled at Mitch.

It was a smile that froze his own response on his lips.

Suzi-q had a beautiful smile.

And a sparkle in her eyes despite the pain. The sparkle was one of peace. It brought a beauty to her he'd not seen in a long, long time, if ever. "You've made peace with God, haven't you, honey?"

She winced in pain at a particularly jarring step the horse took, then nodded slightly. "I've been a fool in many ways. But yeah. I feel wonderful—spiritually at least," she added.

"Well, if you were feeling good with that egg on your head, I'd really have to wonder about you."

"Thinking I'm brainless, are you?" she attempted to joke.

"Only if you said you didn't feel pain," he replied and squeezed her closer.

Her lips curved up slightly, softly, making him realize he was staring at them. His gaze shot up and out into the distance. "Keep your head against me, honey. We'll be there in a minute and we don't want you moving around."

He had been staring at Suzi's lips. Was he crazy?

Shaking his head, he tried to dispel the memory. This was Suzi, his best friend. What in the world had happened? Why would he notice she was pretty and soft and vulnerable as she gazed up at him like that?

Scowling, he realized it had to be all that talk about marriage. He was desperate. That was it. That's why he'd been staring at his best friend as more than a friend. He sure hoped Suzi hadn't noticed. He wouldn't want to hurt their relationship because he made eyes at her.

His mood turned downright dark the closer they got to the ranch house.

"Look, it's Uncle Hawk," Kristina said and waved at Julian.

Mitch glanced up, and sure enough, his youngest brother was standing on the porch. He saw them and Mitch could tell Juls realized something was the matter. He stiffened, then turned and disappeared into the house. "That's right, Kristina. Looks like Uncle Zach is gonna get to see you riding in on Thunderbolt."

"All right!" Kristina said and grinned with glee.

"You're turning my daughter into a terror, Mitch McCade. I can see it now," Suzi whispered, "she's gonna be insisting that she ride everywhere by herself."

Mitch forced out a chuckle. "Better that than fear the horses."

Mitch glanced back up to see Zach, Freckles, Julian and finally Laura come rushing out of the house. "Get ready, Suzi-q. Here they come."

Chapter Seven

Suzi groaned and turned her face into Mitch's chest.

Automatically, Mitch's arm tightened around her, as he guided the horses into the yard.

Red, the manager, came out of the men's quarters, saw what was going on and shouted for some help. Everyone knew Red. Red was always there when he was needed.

Red. Mitch had no idea if that was the old man's real name or simply a nickname because of the bristly red hair that covered his head and face. Still, it didn't matter. He was nearly family. "Red, can you see to these horses?" Mitch called out.

"Sure 'nuff, Mr. McCade."

"What happened?" Julian asked coming forward, pushing past Zach to take charge of the situation.

"A mishap. Suzi slipped in the rain and banged her head. She'll be fine," Mitch murmured. "Can you slide down, honey?" he asked gently.

"I'm fine, really."

She wiggled and pushed away from Mitch. Mitch felt empty and cold when he let her go. He watched her as she eased down carefully. And nearly said something he would have regretted when she went white again.

"Watch out, Juls," Mitch said, and swung down as fast as he could.

"I've got her," Julian replied and with one swift move, swept Suzi into his arms. "You really did a job on yourself, didn't you, Suzi?"

"It was a beginner's mistake. Sloppiness," she muttered.

"Freckles, let's get her upstairs and check her out."

"Be careful. She has a large bump on the back of her head. She was out for nearly a minute."

Julian nodded and started off.

"I'm not that bad," she said to everyone in general.

Mitch simply looked at Zach. Then he turned to Kristina. "You wanna go have some hot chocolate with Aunt Laura, honey?"

Kristina, who was just dismounting, looked uneasily after her mother.

"She'll be fine. Let's go have some hot chocolate and let Julian...er...Hawk examine her and then you can go up to see her, okay Kristina?"

Finally Kristina nodded. Going over to Laura she touched her tummy. "Can I feel your baby move while we wait?"

Laura replied, "I think he's asleep."

"He'll probably wake up. Hot chocolate is warm and it'll make him wake up."

Mitch looked at Zach for a translation of that one but Zach simply shrugged. "Kids have their own logic. Let Laura get Kristina changed and we'll get you changed while we talk.''

Mitch nodded. Since Julian was with Suzi, Zach wasn't going to let him escape without an explanation. That was Zach, brother most of the time, but father more often. Mitch walked up the steps to the porch. Exhaustion was suddenly a heavy emotional burden that sat like a tree trunk right across his shoulders, tense with the effort to keep Suzi still as they'd ridden. Pulling open the screen door he strode into the house.

Turning down the long hall he headed to Zach's bedroom. They both walked in silence through the adobe-style ranch house. The cool air blew in, chilling Mitch. He wondered if Suzi and Kristina were chilled, too.

''Ready to talk?'' Zach asked as he entered the room.

Mitch glanced around. Zach's room had certainly changed since he married Laura. The large four-poster bed was still set against the wall and the chest and dresser

were in their places. But on top of the
dresser were creams and lotions and hair-
brushes—and a gun belt. "Doesn't Laura
know better than to leave stuff like that lying around?" He scowled.

"Don't worry, little bro, your deputy
sheriff's gun is locked up tight in the
desk."

Mitch went to the dresser and fingered
the belt, noting the empty holster. "Is she
still practicing, as far along as she is?"
Mitch asked.

"She's your deputy. Why not ask her?"
Zach drawled.

Mitch simply shook his head. "We're
gonna have to have a talk," he muttered.

"Upset her and you'll answer to me."

Mitch scowled again.

"Pax." Zach grinned and pushed the
door closed. "Now, why don't you stop
avoiding the subject and tell me what happened out there?"

Mitch released the catches on his shirt
and pulled it out of his pants. "Silly woman
stepped into the stirrup without tightening
her cinch."

He kicked off his boots and stripped down to his bare skin. After going over to Zach's drawers, Mitch started digging in them without asking permission. He'd done this so many times it wasn't uncommon to Zach.

"That's not what I'm talking about," Zach said, strolling forward, cleaning out Mitch's pockets and then tossing Mitch's clothes into the bathroom tub.

"Oh?" Mitch asked, turning slightly. He slid into a pair of jeans and then pulled on a green shirt. He pulled on a pair of socks, then stared when he realized they weren't Zach's.

Zach chuckled. "Other drawer. Laura keeps her stuff in that one now."

"Oh." He dropped them back into the drawer, blinked, shoved the drawer closed and opened the other one. After snatching a pair of Zach's socks, he sat down on the bed to put them on.

"We went to the pond. Suzi fell. We rode back and Julian is checking her out. What else is there?" Mitch asked, as he slipped first one sock on and then the other. The more he thought about it the madder he got.

"What happened to put you in a bear of a mood, maybe?" Zach asked mildly.

Mitch stood. "I'm not in any mood. I got caught out in the rain. I'm wet. I'm cold. And a friend nearly knocked her brains out over some stupid beginner's stunt. She knows better." He thought about what happened and started pacing. Seeing her lying there had shaken him. "You'd have tossed me back on the horse to teach me a lesson if I'd done that."

Zach simply waited.

That was one of the traits Mitch hated most about Zach. He could outstare them all. Even now, as old as they were, that stare made Mitch want to come out swinging. There had been many a time he'd done that. He'd learned however, that no matter how angry you got, how upset with the need to lash out, sooner or later you had to make up because family was family. They didn't disappear from your life.

Most of the time.

The flash of his parents' faces deflated

his anger. "I'm just worried, Zach. You should have seen her. She was white."

"I've seen her that way a couple of times before," Zach said quietly.

"Yeah well, this time was worse," Mitch muttered. Blood pressure went right back up.

"Why?" Zach asked and moved to grab a towel. He tossed it to Mitch who rubbed it over his head.

He hadn't even remembered to dry off, he thought sourly. At least he hadn't been dripping. He wondered if Zach had noticed. "It just was. I don't know. Kristina was there. Because it was raining. She's not a kid anymore! Zach, that could have hurt her bad." He tossed the towel back at his brother.

"Yes. She could have been hurt bad. But Juls will take care of her."

A knock sounded at the door and it eased opened. "You decent, boss?"

Mitch sighed. "Yeah, Laura...*Deputy*. Come on in."

Laura waddled in. "Kristina is sound asleep on the couch. She's exhausted. Afternoon-nap time." With a soft smile she crossed to Zach. "I left some hot chocolate in the microwave, Mitch. Why don't you go get some and warm up?"

Mitch was actually relieved that Laura had come when she had. He had to do something to get his mind off the flash he'd had of Suzi lying there helpless, dead. Why in the world had he thought that? It had to have been the pasty color of her skin. And other things, things like blaming himself for taking off years ago and leaving Suzi here alone to fate, just as he'd raced off to his horse and left her there, alone. Running a hand through his hair, he nodded. "Thanks. I think I'll do that."

This was the easiest escape he'd ever made from his brother. Mitch headed to the door. He paused by it and turned. "You sure are an asset to the family, Deputy," he drawled and then with a wink headed out.

"You know what he's grinning about?" Laura asked.

"Yep," Zach said and slid his arms around his wife, pulling her close. "He's grinning because he thinks your arrival got him out of my inquisition.''

"Zach!" Laura said and smiled up at him. The soft smile curved her lips and softened the look in her eyes. "I've told you before to stop that with your brothers.''

Her voice held no heat. He adjusted her into his arms and then turned so they could look out the window. He leaned down and kissed her on top of the head. "Yeah, well, I've learned from you, darling. I got all the information I wanted without turning it into a yelling match.''

Laura leaned back against him and sighed. "And what did you learn?''

He tightened his arms around her and rubbed his chin against her soft blond hair. How he loved this woman. She was his helpmate, the one God had sent and he thanked God every day for her. "I think my brother has finally woken up and might just realize his feelings for that woman upstairs.''

"Oh?''

He grinned at the surprise in her voice. "Yeah.''

"What makes you think he has that kind of feelings for her? From what I've observed of your brother, he isn't serious about anyone, despite what he says about wanting to find a wife by the Fourth of July party."

"Trust me, love. The look in my brother's eyes today when he told me she was a grown woman told me all I needed to know."

"But what makes you think he loves her?" Laura asked.

"She's the first one he has always turned to when something happens."

Laura still didn't understand. She turned to look up at him. "So?"

Zach reached up and cupped her face with his hands. Stroking her cheeks, he stared down into her beautiful blue eyes. "Mitch won't even come to me with his problems. When Mom and Dad died, it was Suzi who grieved with him. No one is closer to him than Suzi."

"She loves him." Laura said with dawning knowledge.

"Yeah. She has for years." His gaze

darkened momentarily. "I wish Mitch had realized it a long time ago and done something about it."

"Everyone has their own time to grieve and heal, Zach," Laura said softly.

"He's my brother. She's like a little sister to Julian and me," he whispered and pulled her into a tight hug.

"And you want him to heal."

"Yeah. I want him to heal. And when he does, he's going to wake up out of the wasteland he's been lying in and realize he's already given his heart."

"Oh...oh! But the picnic, the bet..."

"Yeah."

"Oh, Zach. I hope it happens before that."

"So do I, darling. So do I."

Zach held her close thinking about his brother and offering up a silent prayer that God would remove the scales from Mitch's eyes, open them and just help him to see what was right before him. Because whether Mitch realized it or not, he was already in love with Suzi. And she was head over heels for him.

Chapter Eight

"**O**uch!"

"Lay still, Suzi. You'll be just fine."

Suzi scowled at Julian and then turned to Freckles who sat on the other side of her. "Is he always like this?"

She winced as Julian again pulled her hair as he braided it.

"No. It's just for you. Usually he just lets the patient's hair hang."

That drew a chuckle from Suzi. "I meant his patronizing attitude."

"Hey!" Julian protested.

"Oh, that," Freckles said, putting away the forceps and sutures before stripping off her gloves. "It's required in Attitudes 101. All doctors must learn how to patronize their patients. Hawk passed with flying colors."

"Yeah, I bet Hawk did," she said, emphasizing Hawk.

"Okay, okay, ladies. I'm never going to live that nickname down, am I?" he questioned in his contralto voice.

"Am I going to get rid of the Freckles nickname?" his wife asked.

Suzi grinned at Susan McCade.

"Nope." Hawk winked at Suzi.

"Then you have my answer, Hawk." Susan rolled her eyes and gave Suzi a see-what-I-put-up-with look.

"Okay, Freckles." Julian had the audacity to grin.

"Um, can I interrupt?" Suzi asked.

"Yes?" Julian said.

"Is my head all finished getting wrapped up like a mummy? I'd really like to lie back down."

Julian's banter fell away and his voice turned serious. "Sure thing, Suzi. You're really lucky. The spot only had to have two stitches. However, because you lost consciousness, I want to keep you here for today. I'll call the school and diner and let them know you can't be in tomorrow. You need at least forty-eight hours to rest. Then there is the ankle. We've got it wrapped, but it'll take a week, maybe two, before you will be able to stand regularly again at your waitressing job.''

"The school isn't going to like me missing two days,'' Suzi said.

"They'd like you throwing up on them less.''

"I'm going to give you something for the pain. But I can't knock you out. I'm going to have Zach wake you every two or three hours, to check on you. We want to make sure everything is okay. If you start throwing up, your headache increases or you have problems with vision or speech, I want you to call me immediately, okay? Freckles or I will come right over.''

Suzi sighed. "Okay. Fine.''

Freckles reached out and touched Suzi's hand. *"Por favor, Señorita,"* she said softly.

Surprised, Suzi's eyebrows went up—an action she instantly regretted. "You speak Spanish?"

It was only then she realized she and Julian had lapsed into Spanish as they spoke not even thinking if Freckles could speak the language or not.

"Some, yes. Don't be embarrassed, Suzi. Believe me, if I were embarrassed over every accident I'd ever had, I'd never get any work done. These things happen."

Suzi sighed and then wilted in relief as Julian lowered her back to the pillows. "I know. Still, I've ridden horses forever..."

A knock at the door drew their attention. Suzi waited hoping—and was grateful when it was Mitch who entered. She was in his old room. She had been here many summers when they'd played cards. When he had the measles, she'd sneaked in through the window—and ended up sick a week later. Julian had deposited her right here, which had made her more at ease. The familiar surroundings, the essence of Mitch in all of the mementos on his wall gave her peace.

She had missed his arms around her from

the time Julian had lifted her from them. This was only a small solace. Seeing him, however, eased the rest of the tension from her and she relaxed into the bed. "Where's Kristina?" she asked.

Mitch lifted a thumb, motioning over his shoulder. "Asleep on the sofa. If you want her in here, maybe later. Juls?" he asked, looking at his brother.

"She'll be fine in a day or two."

Mitch nodded. Except he was turning red—a warning sign she'd learned well over the years. She hoped poor Julian wasn't going to get the third degree over the bandage on her head.

Suzi accepted the pills Julian gave her.

Mitch refocused on her. His gaze went to her head, her face, touching every part of her. "If you ever pull such an all-fired stupid stunt again, Suzi, I swear I'll take you over my knee myself!" His voice snapped out like a whip, low, warning and very serious.

Freckles gaped.

Suzi nearly choked on her pills.

Julian's shock showed in his voice as he began, "Now, Mitch—"

"You weren't there Julian," Mitch interrupted, slashing his hand through the air in a shushing motion. "Woman, you could have been killed. Then what would have happened to Kristina?"

"Mitch!" Julian froze staring at his brother in complete shock.

Suzi glared at Mitch even as her insides cried out in pain. "I don't believe that is any of your business, Mitch McCade." Forcing her voice to remain steady, she stuck her chin out in defiance.

He didn't heed the warning sign. "Oh? You have someone else to watch out after her?"

"As I said, it's not your concern. But yes, I do."

Mitch actually looked surprised.

"That's enough, brother," Julian warned and started forward. "She's my patient."

"Well, at least you thought of that. Next time remember you aren't a kid anymore," he said to Suzi, ignoring Julian.

Julian grabbed Mitch by the arm.

Mitch jerked away. "What do you want, Juls? A fight?"

Julian shook his head. "Not at all. I want you to leave and we'll talk later."

"I can manage that," he muttered, and with one last comprehensive look at Suzi, he turned and strode from the room.

Suzi fell back against the bed, no physical pain obvious in her face, though her heart bled from shock.

"I don't believe that. I'm sorry, Suzi. Mitch isn't normally that shakable." Julian moved back to her side but didn't touch her as Freckles readjusted the covers and checked her bandage and wrist before standing.

Suzi lifted a hand. "He was worried about Kristina. He loves her, you see, and knows what it'd mean if he lost her."

She saw the look Freckles and Julian exchanged. Julian moved forward and eased onto the edge of the bed. "He cares about you, too, dear. I think his explosion was because of your injury."

He'd practically accused her of being a bad mother, not to mention making her sound like a wild child. She knew Mitch didn't mean it, but that had hurt more than anything. How many hours, months, years had she given up to be a good mother for her daughter? How many hours had she worked at thankless jobs, shunned by most, as her bosses watched to see if she made any mistakes that could constitute grounds for her termination. She had to work harder, fend off more advances, and have no social life because of her past; all for her daughter so she wouldn't be shunned by those same people that looked down their noses at her. She could not—would not—let them find fault in her actions. "It's okay, Julian. I'm used to Mitch's explosions, though they usually aren't directed at me."

She could see Julian shaking with his effort to control his temper. She smiled. "Really. Don't worry, Julian. He'll get over it."

"Will you?" Freckles asked softly.

"I always do," she whispered and then she turned her head, closing her eyes. Last time she'd been this hurt Kristina had been the result. She was older now and knew whom to turn to when she hurt. And it wasn't Mitch or any other man, or woman for that matter. It was her Heavenly Father. His gentle touch healed all wounds. He had before.

It wasn't simply Mitch's words that hurt, however. It was what was behind his words. Any feelings of attraction she'd felt on the ride back had most assuredly been one-sided. Her hope of maybe attracting Mitch's attention died as she admitted with a sinking feeling she really never would have a chance at his heart.

"I think I'll sleep now," she whispered.

Julian touched her forehead gently and Freckles stroked her hand, before they quietly slipped from the room.

The tears didn't fall until the hall door closed behind them.

Chapter Nine

❦

"Crazy. Unbelievable," Suzi muttered, staring in disbelief at the message that had just been delivered to her. *"Perros!"* she said, referring rather unchristianly to the people who had fired her.

At least her daughter had left for school already and didn't see how upset her mommy was at the moment, she thought, with just a bit of guilt. She tossed down the letter in disgust and started across the room. "Why?"

Stopping, she turned and strode back to the sofa and snatched up the sheet of paper.

"Why, God?"

Staring at the paper, she thought how neatly typed it was. She could tell it had been typed on her own paper at school. The office had a special watermark in the corner—which was present on this letter.

Focusing, she read the words again:

Dear Ms. Fletcher
Due to recent events and questionable activities, we're enacting our morals clause…

She couldn't go on. "Questionable activities!"

Shaking her head, she crumpled the paper once again in her hand. "How can they say this? I only rode with Mitch. For pete's sake, Laura was in the house the entire time I was at the ranch house."

Morals. Dropping to the sofa she glanced back at the wadded up piece of paper before throwing it at the door in frustration. "Oh, Father," she whispered, "what else can go wrong?"

How could they fire her? What was she

going to do? She barely made ends meet, living from paycheck to paycheck.

Leaning forward she dropped her forehead to rest against her hands and sighed. Her head was pounding and she still walked carefully, though she was doing much better than only a few days ago. But to add these ridiculous innuendos on top of everything else...

With a huge sigh, Suzi wondered if she could put off the bill for the new clothes Kristina had needed, or the one for when she'd bought her school supplies. Both were due in a week. Both bills had been paid on time thus far. Both would have been paid off next month—before this.

Mr. Winter would love for her to ruin her store credit. He had only given her an account because she'd put down Zach's name as a reference.

She felt like crying until she remembered that God told her in His Word to trust Him in good times and bad times—simply to trust that He was in control.

The sound of a car outside drew her attention. "What now?" she muttered. Carefully, she eased up and padded across the floor to her door. She pulled the door open just as the person hit the doorbell. She did all she could not to reel in shock.

Standing before her was the worst possible "what now" she could have imagined. "Noble?" she managed to croak out from her suddenly dry throat. In all of the years since the incident, she had never expected him show up at her door. Anyone but him.

She was suddenly seventeen again, afraid, alone, hurt and upset—and all because she'd allowed herself to turn to this man in her own anger and hurt.

"Morning, darling. Why not invite me in?"

Her head spun. What was he doing here? It had to be that he was up to no good. Noble was full of no-good intentions. He thrived on trouble. Trouble was what gave Noble his high. Some men preferred drugs, alcohol and other vices. Though she was certain Noble had tried all of the other vices, the real kick he got was manipulating others and ruining their lives.

If she didn't invite him in, he could expose her own secrets. Her stomach turned and twisted into a tight ball of nausea as the old feelings of helplessness rose. Bracing herself she asked the question, if she did invite him in, just for a moment, what would be the consequences?

She did know one thing for certain. At least he wouldn't be standing on her front porch step.

Moving back, she stood aside. "Come in."

"That's more like it, sugar."

His voice oozed sweetness which made her skin crawl. How could someone so full of meanness sound so nice, be so attractive—at least outwardly. Tall, dark hair, and the lean body that had attracted so many women—still in perfect shape, though she noted he sported new age lines around his eyes and mouth that hadn't been there when he'd been sent away. His dark eyes and good looks captured everyone's attention. When Noble wanted to be, he was very charismatic—in his looks and in his actions. But if a person gazed deeply into the man's eyes they'd see his gaze wasn't full of love and hope like most, but deception and calculation. Intelligence shone in them as they watched, assessed, sized a person up for any weakness.

And Noble knew her weakness.

He'd used it on her before.

"What do you want, Noble?" she asked now, pushing the door closed behind her.

She had an awful feeling he was here to use the weakness against her again. *Why now? Why now? Please just make him leave...*

With a sinking feeling she knew that wouldn't happen. Noble was back. And for some reason, he was here to cause trouble.

The sweet gentle voice of her Heavenly Father floated up within her, reminding her to trust Him.

"What? No offer of coffee?"

She swallowed and reminded herself to stay calm and just brave her way through this meeting. "You know I don't drink coffee. Only tea."

"Ah, that's right." He smiled and strolled across the room before sprawling in a nearby chair. "So, how's life been treating you, sugar?"

"Just fine." Suzi moved across the room to grab a basket of clothes. Striding back, she dropped into a nearby chair and started folding. Working to appear nonchalant, Suzi waited to hear what he had to say.

"You didn't talk to me in church the other day."

His gently chiding voice teased at her, asking her to play his game.

Instead, she tread carefully, working to skirt his game and yet keep him pacified. "You weren't there to talk to me."

"I always want to talk to you, sugar. You know that."

Suzi didn't comment that a few years ago he'd made sure not to be seen anywhere near her, even up until a year ago when he'd been arrested. Instead, she continued to fold her clothes. "I'm sure, Noble. But I've been busy raising my daughter."

"Ah, yes. I saw her in school last week. A cute little thing."

Suzi paled. Dropping the shirt she had just picked up, her gaze shot to Noble's.

He'd seen her daughter. Of course, she knew he probably saw her around town, but at school? Cold chills skittered down her spine. "Yes. She is."

Despite the chills, sweat gathered on the back of her neck.

"I heard you lost your job."

Noble crossed his jean-clad legs and fingered a nearby tasseled lamp, his attention seemingly distracted. Suzi knew better. Very carefully, she replied, "I'll find another one. It wasn't that important."

"My dad can use an assistant housekeeper."

Suzi's entire body turned cold. "I don't need any help, Noble," she said firmly.

His steely gaze cut to her. "So, sugar," he drawled, his gaze pinning her to her chair, "how is your little daughter doing lately? Has the sheriff been spending much time with her?"

"And my daughter is just that, my daughter. There is no claim of a father on the birth certificate."

"From what I hear, the sheriff is looking to get hitched. I'm wondering just how interested he'd be to have some of the local gossip on the different women in town.''

She knew exactly what he meant. Noble planned to tell Mitch just who was her daughter's father. She couldn't let him do that. Too much had happened, too many things between the Mastersons and the McCades. When everyone had deserted her, Mitch and his family had stood by her. But to lose them now, especially when she had thought it might just be possible... It'd ruin her daughter's life to find it out and then lose her "Uncle" Mitch and "Uncle" Zach.

She had always known this was a possibility. This wasn't the first time Noble had held this up. But it was the first time he'd used it to force her into a situation like this.

"You know, Noble. That hate inside you is going to eat you up. I don't know why you feel you have to destroy the McCades.''

Noble's gaze turned ugly. "He sent me away. His daddy caused much of my daddy's problems—''

"Stop it," she began. Suzi wished now

she hadn't said anything. A mean Noble was a dangerous one. "I'm not invol—"

A knock on the door interrupted her, giving Suzi a short reprieve. "Excuse me," she said and stood, going to the door and jerking it open—then wishing she hadn't. Mitch stood there, a frown on his face.

"Suzi, hon, I just…" Mitch's frown changed into a scowl of anger. "What is *he* doing here?"

And she had thought it couldn't get any worse. Tension in the room soared to a new height.

Mitch started forward.

Noble grinned, egging Mitch on.

Suzi placed a hand on Mitch's chest. The snapping anger in Mitch's eyes to find his worst enemy in his best friend's house worried even her. She knew how much Mitch hated Noble.

"I won't have him here harassing you, too. He might get away with it because others won't complain, but I'm throwing him out right now, Suzi."

She had to stop him. Noble would certainly tell what he knew if she didn't.

As if on cue, Noble said, "I only stopped by to check on Suzi and her child. I heard she'd lost her job."

"Get out," Mitch stated flatly. The steely gaze in his eyes warned that even though he was a law enforcement officer, he'd forget that right now just to get this man out of Suzi's house.

"I've offered her a job," Noble added.

Suzi felt the muscles on Mitch's arms bunch. "Please, Mitch," she whispered.

"A job? You! Why, you..." he said, ignoring her very presence in front of him. Suzi knew she had to do something before Mitch's anger at this man finally unleashed and lost him his job. Why oh why had she been so stupid so many years ago? Why couldn't Noble just stop hating this family? Why couldn't Mitch just let it go like Zach now did?

"I've told him I'll be out tomorrow to apply for the job!" Suzi couldn't help it. She had to stop Mitch and that statement would certainly turn his attention.

Mitch's gaze shot to hers. "You what?"

The anger and shock in his eyes pierced

her. Nervously, she swallowed and then stepped back. With as nonchalant a shrug as she could manage she said, "The school decided they didn't need me and Mr. Masterson needs someone to help his staff. It pays well, doesn't it?" she said pointedly at Noble.

With a self-satisfied grin, he nodded. "Better than her old job."

Her stomach churned at the smile.

"I see."

Her gaze went back to Mitch's. The look of betrayal in his eyes nearly undid her.

"I'll be out tomorrow then, Noble."

Thankfully, he took the hint and moved toward the door. Suzi stepped forward between the two men, blocking any contact that might happen. She should have known better. As Noble reached the door, he reached out and stroked her cheek. "Tomorrow."

Mitch stiffened.

She leaned back slightly in warning.

Noble strode out the door, closing it snugly behind him.

Mitch immediately stepped away from

Suzi, causing her to lose her balance. She hadn't realized she'd been leaning against him that hard. She was grateful when he caught her. As angry as he was, she wouldn't have been surprised if he'd watched her fall.

She pulled from his grip and glared up at him. "Don't you dare start with me, Mitch McCade," she warned, her eyes narrowing.

He strode across the room and tossed his hat on a nearby table. Whirling, he faced her squarely. "You aren't going to work for those people."

Suzi thought she well agreed with that. But Noble had a secret he held over her. If only she could blurt it out and get it over with, but Mitch would surely hate her if he knew the truth.

"I need the job," she returned, hiding her despair behind her anger. "And I know the sheriff's department isn't hiring."

"I'd make a place for you before you go working for that family."

Doubling her fists, she seated them on her hips. "Don't even think it, Mitch McCade. I can make it on my own."

"Well, you don't need to, not with that family," he growled and strode across the room to the front window. He shoved the curtain back and stared out as Noble pulled away in a brand new car that had certainly cost his daddy a pretty penny. The engine hummed as he turned it toward the east and headed away.

Eventually, the sound faded, but still Mitch stood there. What was he feeling? Suzi nibbled her lip. His shirt stretched taut over his broad shoulders. At the moment, he looked so unyielding, so unapproachable.

Blast Noble and his father for putting Zach and his brothers through so much as they were growing up. Why oh why had the man tried to take everything from Zach and then from Julian as well? Mitch had vowed as sheriff to do what he could to put a stop to the illegal activities and hatred that Bate and his son dealt out. Unfortunately, it looked as if Mitch was now having to face his own emotions with these men and realize that he wasn't as objective as he was supposed to be.

"Mitch," Suzi said, padding quietly forward, "it'll be fine. The job will pay well and it'll be a change from the school if Mr. Masterson even hires me."

"I thought you disliked him intensely."

Laying a hand on his shoulder she stroked it gently. "I do," she replied. If only Mitch knew how much, he wouldn't be so upset. She knew it wasn't Christian to have the attitude she did and she still worked to find peace but...it was slow in coming.

"So what does Noble hold over you that you don't flat-out refuse his offer right up front?"

Suzi shrugged and stroked his arm again looking out with him. She knew he was only blowing off steam with that question. The morning was beautiful, the sun shone brightly. Hot and dry. How she felt at the moment inside. Hot, dry and empty as she contemplated how she would answer Mitch. Years of pain rose up within; her need to open up completely to this man; her fear of opening up completely. Still... "Maybe he's the father of my child,'' she only half joked, gauging his reaction.

It was quick in coming.

Mitch whirled. "That is *not* the slightest bit funny, Suzi. That guy is a jerk. If you were involved with him like that..."

The utter loathing on his face as he tried to come up with a word to describe what he felt made Suzi shake her head. It was always the same. Mitch and she were best friends but there was one area, one deep secret, that she just couldn't share because of his pain in this area—because of her own shame, despite the fact she knew she'd been forgiven. "Don't, Mitch. I'm so tired of all the fighting."

Wrapping her arms around herself, she moved across the room and put distance between them.

"I know you weren't involved with him," Mitch said, as if reassuring himself. "I've been here your whole life. You've never liked him, even when he was sniffing after you."

Suzi shuddered. "No, Mitch. I don't like him. Can we change the subject?"

The sound of booted feet as he crossed the floor toward her echoed reassuringly. Suzi closed her eyes against the tears. This was her best friend. This was the man she loved. She couldn't lose him, too.

Strong hands cupped her shoulders and pulled her back against his solid chest. "I'm sorry, Suzi-q. Because of everything his family has done and the fact he was running that drug ring…" He sighed. His chin came to rest on the top of her head, and he rubbed it over her hair gently. "I just worry about you. You've been through more than many go through in a lifetime and I don't want to see you hurt, honey."

Suzi turned and slipped her arms around Mitch, burying her head in his chest. "I'm sorry, Mitch. Please, let's not fight. I need a job. This job will give me more time with my child right now than the secretarial job did. And maybe, just maybe, God is in this and has a reason He wants me out there. You know, God does care about us."

"Why did they let you go?" he asked softly.

Suzi stiffened in his arms. "It's not important."

"I think it is." Mitch pushed her chin back and looked down into her eyes.

She shook her head but saw, in his gaze, that he suspected the reason. "They've been looking for an excuse, Mitch. The injury was only a good way to hint at moral impropriety."

Mitch growled low. He'd known it. He'd just known it. When Leah had said that morning in her soft voice that she was worried about Suzi, he'd just known.

Pulling the tiny woman back into his arms he hugged her close. *Why, God? Why?* Suzi had been through so much. He felt guilty for getting angry with her. He didn't like Noble. He didn't trust Noble. But that didn't mean he had a right to tell Suzi to stay away from him. It was just that Noble and his father had tried to destroy Zach when he'd first gotten the ranch. Then when Julian had moved back to open the clinic, Noble had made a move on Freckles as well as having some of his men tear up the clinic.

"I'm going to get you a cell phone, honey. If you need anything, I want you to call me."

She stiffened.

"It's the only condition I'll make. Think about it, Suzi. It's not because of you but that I don't trust him. Let me do this for you, okay? At least then, when you're out there applying for that job and if somehow you *are* hired, I'll be able to be there for you."

She hesitated then collapsed against him. "Thank you."

The soft, gentle whisper wrapped its way around his heart, pulling at him, demanding that he take care of this woman. When had she become fragile? His Suzi had always handled everything so well—until lately.

Or maybe he'd only thought she handled everything well, not realizing she was a very lonely woman who didn't have many to lean on.

"You lean on God, don't you?" he asked now.

If she thought it odd that he ask her that when they had been discussing cell phones, she didn't say so. "I try to, Mitch. I got in trouble the first time by not leaning on God. And I still mess up. But I'm trying to learn to lean on Him and trust Him. And let Him heal my heart—like He did the other Sunday."

Mitch nodded. "I worried when you wouldn't go to church with us," he murmured.

"I know. I just couldn't face those people. I went to that weekly Bible study though and my relationship, in my heart, was there."

"You were hiding, though. It was time for healing," he murmured.

"We all have to heal sooner or later," Suzi said softly.

Mitch knew exactly what she meant. He didn't want to go there. He accepted that she was going to do what she wanted to, regardless of how he felt about it. At least for now she would. He planned to keep a close eye on Noble after this.

"About the job..." Suzi began.

Deciding that if he discussed the subject further it would only upset Suzi, he changed the subject. He would find something to bring a smile to her face, something to take her mind off the worry and pain. "Let's not talk about that."

With a slow grin he pushed Suzi back, met her gaze and said, "So, Suzi-q, tell me, who is next on our list for me to try to woo for a wife?"

Chapter Ten

"You sure I look okay?"

Suzi sighed, scooting past Mitch and behind the counter with the dirty dishes loading her arms down. "You look fine, Mitch. Just straighten your tie."

Dropping the plates in the bin, she watched as Mitch hastily rearranged his tie. "You said Tessa likes men with ties?"

Suzi rolled her eyes. "Yes, Tessa likes men with ties. Tessa works with third-graders all day. Anyone looking decent should mean something to her."

"Gee, thanks," Mitch drawled.

Suzi rolled her eyes. She didn't like it at

all that Tessa had agreed to go out with Mitch. Tessa had always said she didn't care for men in uniform. Until Suzi had approached her. Tessa liked animals—all kinds. She was more into studying wildlife than men, or so Suzi had thought.

Leaning back against the counter, she scowled now at Mitch. "Go on over and sit down. Here comes Tessa."

She motioned to the door. Mitch's gaze turned from Suzi to the beautiful young woman walking into the diner. Small, petite, wearing glasses and her brown hair pulled back, Tessa scoped out the diner and found Mitch. With a smile she strode forward. "Good evening, Sheriff."

Mitch held out an arm. "Evening, Ms. Stanridge."

A pang touched Suzi's heart as she watched him escort the woman over to the table where Suzi had placed the menus.

Shoving it aside, she motioned for Meli, a young Chinese woman new to town to take over her section. Going up to Mitch and Tessa, she pulled out her ticket book.

"And what would you like tonight?" Suzi asked.

Mitch glanced up in surprise, hearing Suzi's voice. Lifting an eyebrow at her tone, he said, "Two teas to start with. Is that all right, Tessa?"

Tessa grinned and pushed the glasses back up her nose. "Actually, I wouldn't mind if it's herbal tea."

Mitch nodded.

"Coming right up." Suzi sauntered off.

"So, Tessa, how is life in Hill Creek treating you?"

Rust brown eyes widened at the question, beautiful rust brown eyes, not dark like Suzi's but a sherry color. He wondered why he'd noticed that. Not many had eyes the color of Suzi's.

She smiled, and her narrow face glowed with enthusiasm warming her entire countenance. "I've found it fascinating, Sheriff," Tessa started.

"Please, call me Mitch."

With a short nod she agreed. "Mitch. I didn't finish telling you the other day in Leah's class…but the kids went out on that field trip, and we found an actual specimen of the horned toad. I had no idea they had those here in West Texas. The children, boys more than girls, were quite thrilled with it.''

"Ah, yes." Mitch had forgotten hearing this story told by Leah. He'd only gotten a bit of it as most of Leah's class had inundated him with questions. "I remember now," he said politely.

"Great. Well, as I was telling Leah, we got it back to class and well, boys at that age can be wonderfully inventive. I couldn't help but laugh when I discovered our latest specimen leaping around the room with a clay shell strapped to his back. The kids had decided he was a mutant.''

Musical laugh spilled out and Mitch chuckled. It reminded him of some of the pranks he'd done as a child. "Curiosity is wonderful. Do you like kids—'' Mitch began.

"Here we go!"

Startled, Mitch glanced up to find Suzi there with the tea. He fell silent as Suzi set the drinks down in front of them, though Tessa didn't slow her string of words.

"Suzi! I was so sorry when Leah told me you'd lost your job. It's just such a shame. We'll all miss you. How are you feeling, by the way?"

Suzi smiled politely. "Just fine now, Tessa. Just fine." Pulling out her pencil, she glanced back at Mitch, her eyes twinkling. "Are you two ready to order?"

Mitch realized he hadn't even looked at the menu. He knew what they served, though. "I'll have tonight's special."

"Oh, no-no-no, Mitch. You can't do that!"

Surprised, Mitch glanced at Tessa. "I— um, excuse me?"

Tessa laughed. "Oh, forgive me. What I meant was, haven't you heard the latest studies on shellfish? Much too high in bad cholesterol causers. Just goes to show you, we shouldn't be eating those things anyway."

Thoroughly confused, he looked at Suzi for guidance. "How about steak, then?"

"Steak isn't good for you either," Tessa added.

"What would you like, Tessa?" Suzi broke in, to Mitch's great relief. He was absolutely stunned that the woman was telling him what to eat and not eat and just not quite sure how to handle it.

"I don't go out much. I usually have a fresh green salad with cucumbers and carrots though, when I do. Plus your soup of the day, provided it's not a creamed soup or full of meat. And then a baked roll. Don't add the butter, please."

Mitch's gaze widened increasingly as he listened to the woman order. "You don't like the food here?" Running a finger around his suddenly tight collar he thought this was the biggest mistake he'd made in a while. He should have asked her if this place was okay for dinner.

"Oh, no, it's not that," Tessa disagreed.

Mitch looked to the beautiful dainty woman in query waiting for an answer.

"I'm just a firm believer in not eating anything that was once a living roaming creature. So I usually grow my own food."

He heard a snort.

His gaze shot up to the perpetrator, but Suzi had a hand over her mouth coughing.

"Are you okay?" Tessa asked, concern creasing her brow.

"We don't get many vegetarians in here, Tessa. I had no idea—"

Tessa smiled sweetly. "That's why I take my lunch to school. I mean, it's no problem for me if others aren't—vegetarians, that is. I just can't imagine clogging my arteries and natural healing system up like that."

Mitch sank down slightly in his chair.

"So, what do you do about going out to eat and such?" Suzi asked.

Smiling, she winked at Mitch. "I just don't go out unless some handsome man asks me."

Mitch realized this was going to be a long night. What had he gotten himself into? He remembered seeing Tessa around. She bristled with constant energy. She liked kids. She was a nice woman. But this?

"Mitch?"

"Huh?" Glancing up, he found both women staring at him.

"I asked you what you'd like to eat."

Mitch looked at the waiting Tessa, then up to Suzi, who had asked the question. "I'll have what she's having."

"Oh, good choice, Sheriff!"

"Yeah," Suzi drawled. "Good choice."

With pad in hand, Suzi scooped up the menus and left. When she was out of earshot, Tessa reached over and touched his hand.

Mitch jumped. Glancing up, he found a soft smile on her face. "I guess we just don't click, do we, Sheriff?"

Relieved, Mitch sank into his chair. "I like kids. I'm looking to settle down and have a family..."

"As am I," she agreed.

"But..."

She grinned. "Yes, but..."

Mitch chuckled. "Let's just eat our meal and have a nice evening, shall we?"

"I'd truly enjoy that. I can't stay out long, though." Removing her hand, she placed the napkin in her lap as Suzi returned. "I tend several different animals at my home. My baby chicks have just hatched.''

Suzi set the bowls before them and left. He thought he saw a look of surprise or pain in her eyes but wasn't sure. Curious.

''Mitch?''

''Huh? Oh, yes. Baby chicks. You have baby chicks?''

''Yes, I do. You see, in Brea where I lived out in California we didn't have wildlife. It's been such a pleasure to be able to raise anything I want here. Each animal is so different, so new, so fascinating to watch.''

''I grew up with chickens,'' Mitch said, wondering if he'd ever been this excited over a chicken...no, he couldn't remember a single time.

''I envy you, Mitch McCade. That's why I moved out here. I want to experience the life of a small Texas town.''

''Well, let's eat up,'' Mitch offered now, and picked up his fork. ''I should get home to my own chores soon as well.''

''Great.'' After a quick prayer, Tessa

Stanridge picked up her fork and began to eat.

That was the longest half-hour meal Mitch had ever sat through. As he was leaving, he motioned to Suzi his good-byes.

After dropping Tessa at her house, he headed out to his own ranch. Located farther on down the road past Zach's, it was on the property that had once, when Mitch was no more than a babe, belonged to Bate Masterson. Funny how he'd ended up the one with the land.

Turning down the long, dark driveway, he pondered now about his date tonight. Was he that desperate that he'd want to marry someone like Tessa?

Granted, Tessa was a wonderful woman, but so alien to what he thought all women to be like. Take Suzi for example. Now there was a typical woman. She worked, raised her child, and went to church, though she had hidden away as much as possible. But she loved God. She could sit down and have a rare steak with him or a salad the next day. She never once reacted like Tessa had toward his meal.

How did the woman survive out here in a world so different?

Shaking his head at the oddness of it, he pulled up to his ranch house and killed the engine. The housekeeper had left a light on in the living room.

He had told her not to cook because he was going out tonight. She came out daily to clean his house, cook a meal and see that the ranch hands saw to the cattle, except on the weekends when she was off.

It was one concession to his isolation he'd allowed. He cooked some, but preferred having a meal ready when he got home. He just couldn't drop by Zach's anymore with him married, nor Julian's for that matter. Also, some nights, because of his job, it was late. He'd found this arrangement best.

Climbing out of the four-by-four now, he reached up and loosened his tie. Slipping his hands into his jeans pockets, he gazed up at the stars. "What am I really looking for, God? What type of woman? I thought I knew—until tonight. I'm just not sure...."

The distant sound of a vehicle drew his

attention. Down the long stretch of highway he saw a car turning onto his road. He wondered if Zach had come out this way or Julian. Was Laura okay? Had the baby come? No, they'd have called him on his radio.

So he waited.

It was only as the car got closer he recognized the sound of the engine. "Suzi."

A slow smile kicked up the corners of his mouth as her car approached and then pulled up beside him. When she shut down the engine, all was quiet. Even the sound of the crickets was gone. The only noise was the distant echoing of the engine's former roar.

Mitch leaned back against his vehicle and crossed his ankles. With a smile, he watched Suzi climb out of the car.

"So what brings you here this time of night, Suzi-q?"

She looked tired, still in her stained uniform. Her hair had escaped, slipping down around her face in soft, dark, damp curls that were almost dry from the long drive. The light near the barn cast just enough light for the shadows on her face to stand out starkly, making her look mysterious.

"I wanted to see how your date went."

He chuckled. "Oh?"

Still, Suzi stood by her car, grinning.

She was certainly in an odd mood tonight, he thought. "Wonderful," he lied.

Her deep rich chuckle floated across the distance. "Then why can I hear your stomach rumbling from here?"

That was his Suzi. Shoving away from his vehicle, he closed the distance. "I didn't know she was a vegetarian."

"Nor did I, Mitch." Her voice carried a tone of amusement.

"She's a sweet woman." After all, Tessa was, and she would make someone a wonderful wife and gifted mother.

"Yes, Mitch, she is." The soft sound of Suzi's understanding wrapped its way around his heart.

"And though she'll make someone a wonderful wife and mother, she's not for me."

"No, Mitch, she's not."

Why did her words of agreement make him feel good?

Turning, he leaned against the car next to her. "I want to get married."

Suzi shifted and a soft hand touched his arm. "I know you do, Mitch."

The crickets had resumed their song, chirping out their gentle nighttime symphony of celebration. In the distance a dog barked. You could hear the occasional protest of cattle who were settling down for the night.

For some reason, despite all the noise, he felt lonely, empty and lost. "I don't know what I want, Suzi," he admitted now, in the near darkness. "I mean, all my life I have wanted to do what is right, to fit in, to prove that I am acceptable, that I can do a good job..."

"Oh, Mitch," she whispered, and stroked his arm.

Shaking his head, he sighed. "I keep thinking one more thing and it will all be resolved—I'll finally fit where I am supposed to be. You know, I never fit in when Mom and Dad were alive."

"Of course you did, Mitch."

"Not really," he replied. "Zach had our parents and then Julian had Zach, but I— I—"

"You had me."

Those three words stunned him. "Yeah. I sure did, Suzi-q."

"And I had you."

"Not always," he murmured.

The quiet lengthened as they both knew what hung between them—he wasn't there when she got pregnant.

"I brought you something."

Her voice, laced with play, caught his attention.

"Oh?" Turning he tried to see through the shadows into her eyes. "And what would that be?"

Suzi in this mood could be something else.

"Well, seeing as how your latest conquest tried to starve you…"

Suzi's voice trailed off as she turned and pulled open the back door. When she turned back toward him, she had a covered tray in her hands. "Food?" he asked?

She chuckled. "Tonight's special. Since Kristina is spending the night at Leah's, I thought I'd bring this out to you."

"Wonderful!" Mitch said, and reached for it.

"But I might just have to make you wait on it," she added, slipping it out of his reach.

He froze, his hand outstretched. Watching her carefully, he said, "Why is that, ma'am?"

"When you take a woman out, you should always make sure you know more about her than you did with Tessa."

"Your point?"

"Hmm, my point is, if you served this up to Tessa, she'd likely get sick. Now me, on the other hand, I sure wouldn't, as you know."

She sniffed the food. "As a matter of fact, I can't remember the last time I had time to sit down to a meal and have a special like this..."

Mitch chuckled. "Okay, okay, would you like to join me?"

She held the tray out to him. "I'd be glad to."

Turning, she trotted off toward the house. Mitch simply shook his head and followed. Tonight looked to be better after all.

Chapter Eleven

Walking into Mitch's ranch house, Suzi flipped on the light near the door and tossed her apron on the nearby entrance table. Stretching, she headed into the living room and sank down. "You've done more work here in the living room, I see," she commented, glancing around. An old, braided multicolored rug covered the hardwood floors. And not only had Mitch refinished the sofa, but he had sanded and varnished the end tables as well. And there was a new chair.

"New rug and armchair."

Mitch tossed his hat onto the coffee table

in front of Suzi, then set the tray down after shoving the stack of magazines to one side. Moving through the living room and up the small step, he went into the kitchen.

"Where'd you find the new furnishings?" she asked.

"An antique store about an hour north of here."

"I like the rug."

"I'm going to start on the back bedroom in a month or two," he replied. He came back into the living room with two plates, cups and silverware. Dropping them onto the table, he sat down next to her and poured them both a soda.

"Umm, thanks Mitch," she murmured. "I was only kidding, however. You don't *have* to feed me. I still have to drive back."

"Which is exactly why I *am* going to feed you. It's a long drive."

"Actually, I'm seriously considering stopping by Zach and Laura's to spend the night. Leah is supposed to bring Kristina out there early tomorrow. We're going to work on a special baby project with Laura."

"What's that?"

"Painting the crib." Suzi chuckled.

When Mitch pulled back the cover and started dishing up his plate, Suzi leaned forward and filled her own. "I'm starved."

"Me, too." Looking at each other, they burst out laughing.

"Oh, Mitch, that was so awful. I wish you'd seen the look on your face when you realized you and she couldn't agree on what to eat."

Ruefully, Mitch grinned. "I was pretty stunned."

"You looked like you'd lost your best friend!" Sitting back, she bowed her head, then ate. "I'll not forget it anytime soon."

Mitch, who cut a piece of fried fish, paused to wave the knife at her. "Don't laugh. You were the one snorting about it."

"I don't snort!"

He grinned and poked the fish in his mouth. "You did then."

"Mitch McCade," Suzi said. Shaking her head, she finally gave in. "I have something else I want to talk to you about, too."

"I knew it. This was too far to drive just for this."

Suzi giggled. "I couldn't very well ask you in front of everyone. Laura wants you to do her a favor. Tomorrow Freckles and I are going to help her paint the crib and do baby things. Zach has promised to stay away. He's going to take Angela shopping for her spring dance."

Mitch snorted. "Wonder if he'll be able to handle that?"

"Now, come on. Since Laura has arrived, he's gotten much better at helping Angela with things like that. He's learned. I'd like to see *you* shop for a teenage girl."

"*I* don't have to shop for a teenage girl," he replied. "Go on. What do you need?"

Suzi savored the food. She knew Mitch was going to blow a gasket when he heard what she wanted. "Laura bought a new horse for Zach as a birthday present."

Mitch nearly choked on his fish. "She what?" Swallowing, he shook his head before clearing his throat again. "She's not supposed to be around horses as far along as she is."

"I know. I know. But the man is going to deliver it tomorrow and Laura needs your help. She wants to put some special things up in the stall where Sierra used to be. Since the mare had to be put to sleep, Laura thought a new stallion for Zach to work with and train would thrill him."

"He was looking at a nice one not too long ago."

"Laura knows that."

Suzi grinned at Mitch's look. "It's not that horse is it?"

Slowly, she nodded. "Yep. She said she also plans to breed Jingle Bells with him. Make the horse calm down, she swears."

Mitch groaned. "I should have known. That horse. It's going to be the end of her. They're both stubborn females…"

"Will you help?"

Mitch glanced askance at her. "If it'll keep Laura away from the stables, you know I will. Why didn't she ask me herself?"

Suzi grinned and set her empty plate down. "She told me she figured she'd let you give me the lecture about being around horses in her condition and you'll be all cooled down tomorrow when you show up.''

A bark of laughter escaped Mitch's chest. ''Well, that's for certain.''

''And I have to go,'' Suzi said, standing. Picking up her dishes, she went into the kitchen to rinse them. Mitch stood and cleaned up before following her. She took his dishes and rinsed them while he started loading the dishwasher.

''I hope you decide to stay at Zach's. That little extra room is always there if you don't want to wake them. It's just too long a drive to go back tonight, Suzi,'' Mitch said, walking her to the door.

Grabbing up her apron she headed out the door. ''I think I will. I told Laura I might show up tonight. And after that date, I just couldn't resist coming out here to talk with you about it…''

''And ask me to do Laura a favor.''

''Hey, after that date, I figured I could get you to do anything.''

''You had a hand in setting me up with her. I could have said no.''

Suzi stopped beside her car. "But you wouldn't."

Mitch pulled open her door. "And how can you be so sure?"

Smiling cheekily, Suzi said, "'Cause any woman would look safe to you after what you went through with Tessa!"

She squealed with laughter when Mitch gaped. "Oh, yeah?"

Before she could react, he'd scooped her up and spun her around. "Safe, are you? I wouldn't call that safe."

She held on, laughing as she did every time Mitch did this. She'd known it was coming when she threw that comment out at him. This felt so nice except, instead of being fun this time, it was more disconcerting.

Mitch slowed and stopped and dropped her legs. "You, my dear woman, are about the least *safe* woman I know."

His arms around her held her loosely like they had a thousand times before, but this time something was different. This time as Mitch gazed down at her, his teasing gaze changed as his eyes touched on every part of her face. Slowly, his arms tightened.

Suzi felt the change, yet couldn't believe it. Automatically she leaned into him as his arms drew her closer.

The slamming of a door down in the workers' quarters had him jumping back like he'd been shot.

"Well, I'll see you tomorrow then," he said quickly.

Disappointed but not surprised, Suzi nodded. What had she been thinking? That he would actually kiss her? "'Night, Mitch. Sleep well."

She climbed into the car. The engine roared to life. As she started to back out, she heard, "You, too, Suzi-q. You, too."

Mitch watched her leave. He didn't move until her lights were out of sight. Then he turned and in his anger kicked at a stone. "What were you thinking?"

Shaking his head in disgust he headed toward the house. "She's Suzi. She's off-limits."

After climbing the steps, he strode through the front door. He crossed back to the kitchen and turned out the light. Unbuttoning his shirt, he started toward the back bedroom where he slept. "Of course she's off-limits."

A soft inner voice echoed the one question he'd never asked himself before. *Why?*

"Why?" he said aloud now.

Toeing off his boots, he paused. "Why?"

He shucked his pants before crossing to the bathroom and washing up, the entire time pondering the question. "Well, she is...she's Suzi," he muttered. "She's my friend. She's...I couldn't even *think* of her in that way."

Suddenly he realized that was a lie, because he had been thinking of her in that very way. When he'd held her tonight, he'd held a desirable woman, a beautiful woman, an earthy woman, one who was strong yet vulnerable, determined yet childlike in some ways, soft and yielding, yet able to stand on her own two feet.

Dropping to the edge of his bed, he stared at his reflection in the dresser mirror. "Well, it ends here. Tonight. Just because

I've decided to get married doesn't mean I need to go around looking at *every* woman like that.''

With a shake of his head, he crawled under the covers and stacked his hands behind his head.

But it was a long time before Mitch finally found the solace of sleep. And his dreams were haunted with pictures of a dark-skinned, dark-haired, dark-eyed angel.

Chapter Twelve

"And here he is now."

Mitch heard those words and slowed on the steps. "Morning, Suzi, Laura, Susan."

Susan laughed. "Might as well call me Freckles. I'm afraid it's stuck with the rest, Sheriff."

Mitch grinned at his sister-in-law. "And what are you doing here today with these two?"

Mitch motioned with his hat at Suzi and Laura who sat on the porch in the cool morning breeze. "You, of all people, I wouldn't expect to see conspiring like this," he teased.

Freckles blinked, wide-eyed, her nose twitching. "But I'm the one who suggested it," she informed him.

Mitch shook his head. All three women burst into gales of laughter.

"Look at the bright side, Mitch," Laura said now, managing to push herself up.

"What's that?"

"You're a conspirator, too, so there's no reason to worry."

"Thanks, Laurie."

Laura chuckled. "We just found out the horse won't be here until tomorrow. To keep everything quiet, I've sent most of the men out to the north pasture and the others I sent to help out at Julian's place." She winked at Freckles. "Since Julian isn't there—he's making rounds at the hospital and then heading to the clinic—they can't ask him questions or he them. We have time to get the changes done I want and then have everything ready for when the horse is delivered tomorrow."

"Just what is it you want done, Laura?" Mitch asked now, moving forward and helping Laura down the stairs as she moved toward the barn.

The other two women stood and followed. Suzi dropped in beside him walking quietly, her jeans and light-blue button-down top making her glow today.

"There are some boards to be replaced and I needed a plaque finished and nailed into place—though that'll have to wait until tomorrow, I suppose. And I also wanted you to move some things in the back room out here because I'm making him up a special office. He's been using it on and off for awhile, but I want it to be turned into an official office for him."

"I see we're going to be busy," Mitch murmured and slipped a hand to Laura's elbow as they approached the stables.

"I'm sure we will. I'm looking forward to it, though."

"Aren't we all," Freckles broke in. "Just think. Zach is going to be so surprised. The adventure of it alone will be worth the work."

That was his sister-in-law, Freckles. She loved adventure.

Laura moved into the stable and showed them where she wanted the room. Stretching, she rubbed her sore back. "I didn't sleep very well last night. After we get the crib painted I think I'm going to take a nice cool bath," Laura murmured.

"And a nap," Freckles added. "You're too far along to be working long hours like you did yesterday. While you do that, I'll run to the clinic and then be back to help you set up the rest of the baby's room."

"Great, Freckles," Laura said grinning.

Mitch frowned. "If Julian needs your help, I'll be glad to stay and help Laura, Freckles."

"Not at all. What do men know about setting up babies' rooms?"

Mitch simply lifted an eyebrow at Freckles. "I think I've just been insulted."

Freckles' laughter rang out as she turned and bounced on ahead to talk to some of the horses.

Mitch dabbed at his damp neck, realizing the humidity was up. "Well then, if we're going to get this done, we'd best hurry. Humidity means rain, probably later today."

"Then I'm going around to the back porch if you don't need anything else," Laura said.

Mitch shook his head. "Just be careful."

She only laughed and waddled off. Freckles strolled out after her.

"She's only pregnant, Mitch, not sick."

Mitch turned to Suzi who still stood there smiling slightly. "Maybe. But she looks big enough to have a small cow."

Suzi nodded. "She's at the end of her pregnancy—that's normal."

Mitch moved into the room to start working. "Was that...I mean...did you?"

Awkwardly, Mitch asked the question, realizing he had never really discussed any of this with her before. The surprise on her face showed that she hadn't expected him to start now either.

"I'm out here to help rearrange this room with you for awhile. I offered, telling Laura you'd scalp her if she dared try to work out here."

She moved past Mitch and started gathering up papers.

Curious, and since he'd already opened

that door, he decided to pursue it. "Did you swell like she is swelling, Suzi?"

Suzi paused in her shuffling of papers.

Mitch watched her back closely. Her tiny shoulders hunched as she leaned forward. "No more than normal, I suppose," she finally said.

Mitch moved forward and touched her arm. Leaning against the desk, he seated his hip on it. "Tell me about it."

Suzi's eyes widened with surprise. "About what?"

Why was she so evasive? he wondered. Catching her hand, he pulled her over to a beat-up sofa in the corner. "About your pregnancy and Kristina's birth."

Suzi swallowed. "I—uh—what do you want to know, Mitch? *Why* do you want to know?"

He could tell he had caught her off guard. "In all the years I've known you, we've discussed your mother's feelings about the pregnancy, the fact you were shunned, that the birth happened in the middle of a rainy night. But," Mitch said, shrugging, "I guess seeing Laura and just how uncomfortable she looks has made me wonder how you did it.''

Suzi dropped her gaze, but not before Mitch caught the glimpse of tears.

''Ah *chica*,'' he murmured softly. Reaching out he cupped her cheek. ''You are not as strong as you let on, are you?''

''I'm only human, Mitch. Had it not been for me leaning on God, I never could have survived. No one believed I had repented. I had to pay some price in their eyes.''

''But you don't,'' he said.

''They thought I did.''

''How did you feel about the pregnancy? I mean, you said you didn't swell any more than Laura…''

''What are you asking, Mitch?''

Mitch shook his head. ''I guess I'm just asking how you made it alone, without someone there to hold your elbow or help you up or rub your back, like I've seen Zach do for Laura lately.''

''Sometimes you don't have a choice. You just have to lean on God and accept that when you make a mistake He still loves you.''

Mitch nodded. "Were you as big as she was?" he asked, as he stood and crossed the room to move the old desk and chair and make way for the new ones that Laura had stashed in a back stable. He thought giving Suzi space was the best thing he could do now.

"I was bigger," Suzi said, and the tension drained from her voice. Giggling, she confided, "They kept telling me they thought I was carrying twins I was so big. Do you remember, I was as big as Laura before she was this far along."

"I guess I just didn't notice."

"You were pretty upset when you found out."

"Yeah," Mitch said, remembering now. "I had no right to be, Suzi."

"Sometimes we disappoint each other. That's life. Friends aren't perfect."

"I sure haven't been."

"Parents aren't either."

Mitch stiffened. "Maybe not. I'm gonna go get that other desk now." With a shove, he pushed the old desk out the door.

"You're running?" Suzi called out.

Mitch scowled. "You know very well I am."

Her sweet chuckle floated on the air after him. "I'll make you talk to me about it more one of these days, Mitch McCade. You're going to learn that there's more to life than guilt and anger."

Mitch shook his head as he headed off toward the back stable. Maybe so, but thinking about his parents and how they'd just left him, left them all... He wouldn't ever do that. He could do better. He would do better.

"I won't be betrayed again," he said softly, and went back to work.

Suzi watched him stride off to get the other desk and nibbled her lip in worry. Lately Suzi had noted that Mitch seemed more bothered by what he saw as his parents betrayal. She wanted to talk to him, to make him face it, but even a year ago he wouldn't admit he was angry at his parents, but more angry at himself for failing.

Maybe he was finally starting to realize what the real problem was—that he had never forgiven his parents for their desertion.

Trying to prove something to a dead parent or to himself was useless and empty in the end.

Father, please help him. I don't know what else to do to help him.

And she didn't. To be honest with him would hurt him. Maybe just time would help. In the meantime, she'd work and wait for Kristina to show up. Maybe Kristina would work her magic and get Mitch to open up a bit more.

Shaking her head, she headed back into the office to finish the papers.

Grabbing a hankie, she wiped the perspiration away and then gathered the rest of Zach's ledgers and set them up on a shelf.

Mitch returned and within an hour, he had moved all of the new furniture in and put the old furniture out of sight. Then the two of them worked together in peace to get the office back in order.

"So where is Kristina?" Mitch asked, as they finished up the last of the ledgers.

"I don't know. I expected her first thing

this morning. Leah sure likes her, though. She might have taken her to the park and for ice cream before bringing her out.''

Mitch glanced down at his watch. That was when he noticed how dark it had gotten. Glancing back up, he went to the window and looked out. "Uh-oh.''

Suzi moved up by him. She didn't have to ask. She'd lived in the area long enough to know exactly what Mitch meant by the expression. Without saying anything, Mitch swung around and picked up the phone. He quickly dialed his office. "Hey, Dara, can you give me a weather report?''

Suzi watched him as his features darkened, as dark as the eerily clouded sky outside.

"I'll be there as soon as I can. No, wait. I'd better stay here. Laura and Freckles are out here alone. I don't want to leave them.'' He paused. "Yeah, put out an alert to the ones off duty.''

When he hung up, Suzi moved forward. "Bad?''

He nodded. "Huge cell moving this way. It's touched off several twisters between

Caddola and here. If we'd had the radio or TV on we'd have known something by now."

"I wonder why Laura hasn't said something."

Mitch growled, "She's asleep, probably. I heard a horse earlier and figured it was one of the men coming back early. It was probably Freckles going back to the clinic." Closing the windows and flipping the chest doors closed, he headed out of the office. "Come on. We'd better go check on her."

"Mitch," Suzi whispered, following. "I have to find out where Kristina is. I don't want her caught out on the road in this."

Mitch paused. "Okay, go ahead and call Leah and leave a message. Then leave one with Dara that if anyone spots Leah to let her know."

Suzi nodded. Mitch walked back with her while she called. Suzi knew too well how weather like this could turn ugly in a split second. She'd seen it too many times. After leaving the two messages she turned to

Mitch. "They said they'd keep an eye out for her."

Mitch hesitated, then pulled Suzi into his arms. "It'll be fine. Don't worry."

Suzi hugged him tight, despite how sticky they both were. "Thanks."

Just his voice, his touch was reassuring. With a deep breath, she stepped back. "Okay. Let's go."

The sound of sudden silence as they left the barn stopped them both.

Not a leaf stirred, not a sound, absolutely quiet. And the air was so thick it was hard to breathe. Suzi and Mitch shared one nervous glance before they took off, at a run, for the house.... But they didn't make it before the rain started.

Four steps out into the exposed yard and the sky opened up, proclaiming its fury.

Chapter Thirteen

"Laura!"

The rain muted Mitch's shout as they rushed up the porch stairs.

"I'm sure she's in the house. She wouldn't be out in this."

Mitch only nodded, every muscle in his body tense. He jerked open the door and rushed in, only to slump with relief when he found Laura sound asleep on the sofa.

The thud and grunt behind him distracted Mitch long enough to realize Suzi had run into him. Turning, he stepped aside—and thought she looked like she'd just gone swimming in the nearby creek.

"That water is cold," she said, grabbing at him to balance herself.

The screen door, not completely closed, slammed shut on a vicious swoosh of wind.

Suzi jumped and whirled, grabbing at the door.

"Hmm...." Laura roused on the sofa, shifting slightly as her eyes blinked wearily open. "Mitch?" Laura's sleepy voice jerked his attention back around. Slipping into his professional mode, he strode forward.

"Wha—" she glanced past him, focusing on Suzi and then finally outside. "It's raining."

"Yeah, I'd say so," Mitch drawled calmly. "Pretty nasty."

On cue, the sound of the rain changed as hailstones, mixed with the pounding of the rain, battered the roof and objects not covered outside. "Oh, dear. How many of our men are out in this?" She swung her feet around and sat up.

"They'll take cover in a line shack. Don't worry. Where is Freckles?"

"Not here." Laura shook her head, confirming Mitch's suspicions. "She left for the clinic earlier. Said she'd stop by later. I thought I'd take a nap."

Mitch caught sight of Suzi as she slipped past them and down the hall. In no time, she returned with two towels. "Here," she murmured to Mitch.

Mitch took the towel with a nod and smile to Suzi.

"How long ago did she leave, Laura?" Mitch started drying off, doing his best to wipe the excess water that ran down his neck and arms.

Suzi dried off as she moved to the TV. Grabbing up the remote, she hit the power button and flipped to the local weather station.

"Um..." Laura glanced around, located a clock then sagged. "I've been asleep an hour and a half."

"When did she say she'd be back?" Mitch questioned.

"Oh." Finally waking up, Laura nodded. "No, she wouldn't come out in this. I'm sure she's at the clinic. She mentioned something about surprising Julian so it'll be awhile. He wasn't due out at the clinic until four today.''

"Good.''

"We should go into town,'' Laura said and started around Mitch toward the hall.

"Whoa,'' Mitch said, catching Laura by the arm and stopping her before she'd gone two steps. "Zach would have a conniption fit. No, I think we'd better sit tight.''

"Mitch!'' Suzi's sharp command jerked his head in her direction.

The weather report had a local map up on the screen. Three huge cells nearly covered the entire background of the map. One over in the next county moving their way, one to the east battering their neighbors and the final one just moving into Hill Creek County. The colors of the part of the cell moving their way, however, were dark, indicating possible tornadic activity. Then it flipped to a lightning strike picture. "Lightning strikes and touchdowns all over the place.'' Suzi stood, braced, remote in hand, her gaze not leaving the screen as she studied and calculated the movement of the dangerous storm.

Mitch studied the picture as well. Finally, his mind made up, he said, "Guess that settles it. We're taking you to the cellar, Laura."

Laura, now completely awake, scowled. "Mitch McCade, you aren't my husband and I didn't think you'd act like him. I am perfectly fine. If weather is like this, you know they're going to need the sheriff and every deputy they can get out working the roads. Just think of all the emergency calls they'll be getting."

Mitch started gathering up small blankets and pillows. He went to the closet and pulled out a suitcase that his family always kept packed with important papers for such occasions. "I may not be your husband, but I am your boss and as your boss, I'm not letting you go out in this on duty until the worst sweeps over. As far along as you are, it would be a risk."

Glowering, Laura waddled down the hall. "Very well. Just let me get a few things…" All noise and light within the house ceased, causing Laura to freeze in mid-stride and mid-sentence.

The abrupt lack of electricity made the storm outside sound all the louder—and more menacing.

No one spoke as the sound of the howling wind and crashing of branches outside shouted in a battle of destruction.

"It can wait," Suzi finally whispered. "We should go—now."

Mitch concurred completely. The hairs on the back of his neck were standing up on end. He'd been in storms like this many times before, but now with Suzi and Laura—a pregnant Laura and the feeling of responsibility for them—he wouldn't risk anything happening. "That's right. Come on, Laura."

Mitch strode over and slipped a hand to her elbow.

Suzi rushed forward and grabbed the door.

"Where's Kristina?" Laura suddenly asked.

"Not here, thank goodness. Leah will certainly keep her inside until this blows over."

Mitch saw the worry in her eyes and

wished now he'd encouraged Suzi to go on into town last night. Then she could have picked up Kristina on the way out here and she wouldn't be worrying where her daughter might be. He didn't like seeing her like this.

"Careful on these stairs," Mitch murmured to Laura now, as he carefully escorted her out the door and down the first steps.

Cold, harsh rain pelted them.

Laura sucked in a sharp breath.

"Suzi, honey, can you take this case for me?"

Suzi hurried forward and moved past Mitch, grabbing the suitcase on the way. "Hurry, Mitch. I have a bad feeling..."

Wiping at her face, she turned toward the east side of the house.

"Me, too, honey," Mitch echoed, though he knew she hadn't heard him. The howl of the wind and swoosh of rain was deafening.

Laura glanced around. Over the noise she shouted, "I've not been in a tornado before. Are you sure about this?"

As Laura hurried with Mitch, she raised

a hand to protect her stomach. In the process, she slipped.

Mitch paused, steadying her, taking a moment to brush the water from his face. "We're doing this my way." Taking a breath, before Laura could question what he meant, he bent and with one quick heave, he scooped up Laura.

"Mitch McCade...ouch!"

"Duck your head, woman. It's hailing."

"Mitch, the door—" Suzi's shout reached him. Glancing ahead, he saw Suzi.

She had set the suitcase down and jerked against the heavy door. The wind whipped her hair like ropes wrapping their tentacles of strength around her face. She clawed at them and pulled at the door again.

Mitch reached the cellar on the east side of the house and set Laura down.

"Oh my," she cried out over the noise.

Mitch glanced around and saw what she stared at. The large maple out front swayed, branches touching the ground in the wind.

The sound of metal shrieked. A panel of the chicken coop flew off.

"Hurry," he called out, his voice and

breath snatched on the wind. "Move, honey," he directed to Suzi and with a great yank pulled open the heavy door—and nearly fell off his feet as the wind suddenly stopped.

Suzi's understanding mirrored his own knowledge. "Get in there now!" he commanded and grabbed Laura by the arm, shoving her toward the door.

A low hum filled the still air.

A hum and something else.

Suzi, who had just started down behind Laura, turned and froze. "Oh, no...Mitch! It's Leah."

Mitch whirled.

A white compact pulled up. The car stopped just short of some debris that had already scattered in the long drive. Pushing open the door, Leah slipped out and waved. From here Mitch could see Leah was as nervous as she was happy to see them. Her entire features were bleached white and tension filled her face. At least, he would guess that was what it was. Weather like this was hard for anyone to navigate on the road

"We thought to come on out—" she called out worriedly.

"Leah!" Suzi cried cutting her off.

Mitch's heart dropped to his stomach when he saw the horizontal motion in the distance.

"Kristina!" Suzi started forward.

Mitch snagged her around the waist, pulling her back as he pushed past her.

"Get to safety!"

Hoping she did as he'd ordered, he continued on at a dead run toward Leah and Kristina who had just exited the vehicle and started on their way toward them. But instead of running toward them, Leah froze, then turned and without pause rushed the opposite direction.

"Leah! Stop!" What in the world had gotten into the woman? Mitch nearly stumbled with shock at her reaction.

"Kristina, go to your—"

"I'm here," Suzi shouted. "Kristina, hurry!"

The horizontal cloud rolled, its gentle, beautiful movement slowly drooping as it curved and floated like a feather released upon a soft wind down, down, down until it touched the ground.

Leah didn't see it. She kept running away—away from safety and people.

Mitch rushed on. "Leah!"

Muttering under his breath he pushed hard.

Leah looked back, terror on her face.

That was Mitch's one break in this whole mess. Had she not glanced over her shoulder, she probably wouldn't have slipped on the metal and leaf debris scattered in her path.

But she did and it gave Mitch the extra seconds he needed to catch up with her. Mitch silently thanked God when she went down in the mud. With a leap, he tackled her.

She shrieked. The wind shrieked in agreement as the quiet was suddenly filled with the deceptively gentle rotation that was now closing the distance too fast for his own peace of mind.

Bright lights flared. Power lines snapped faster than he cared to count.

Mitch sank his hands onto the woman's

dress, grabbing at her slick shoulders. "It's a twister, Leah. Stop fighting me!" Shaking her did no good. She continued to claw and resist him. He realized she wasn't going to listen as she continued to scream and fight.

Shaking his head, he stood, forcing himself up and dragging her with him. He wasn't going to stand here and argue with her when they had no time left to argue. He'd drag her to safety—or die trying.

"Mitch!" Suzi, who had reached safety with Kristina, turned back now for him. "Hurry!"

Pressure filled the area. Mitch's ears felt clogged. Breathing was an effort as he dragged Leah.

Suzi saw what was happening and in a sudden spurt of speed, left safety and ran toward them.

Mitch nearly choked with fear seeing her racing from the shelter. "No, get inside, Suzi!" he shouted over the building noise. "Go back!"

A low roar filled the distance. The sound was eerie; different from any other Mitch had heard before. It was the one sound that always struck fear in the people of the Plains, the sound of the destructive winds that were so unpredictable they could destroy a house but leave a shack standing ten feet away.

"Hurry, Mitch!" Suzi rushed up. "Leah!"

Leah still fought, whimpering and fighting no matter what Mitch did. That's why it was such a shock when Suzi reached out and slapped her—hard.

"Look at me!"

Leah did and suddenly, as if jolted out of her fight, she started running toward the shelter.

Mitch didn't question why that had worked, he simply went with it, running right behind her.

Over the roar a crack resounded, lightning flashed and a boom followed.

Suzi cried out.

Mitch was hit from behind and flew forward, just short of the shelter.

Pain exploded.

His heart thudded and he turned to see

Suzi, stunned, on her knees, holding her left cheek.

Acting on pure instinct, he reached for and grabbed her. Without a thought as to what might happen, he shoved her down the stairs. Following her down the stairs, slipping, tripping, sliding, he snagged the rope that was tied to the huge door once everyone made it inside. He didn't bother to lower it quietly. Looking down the mouth of a tornado was not something he wanted to experience.

With a jerk at the end of the stairs, the door teetered. Then with a loud, resounding thud, the cellar door fell down behind them. He tied it off.

Glancing quickly about, Mitch spotted Laura and Leah on the far side of the cellar. Laura was comforting Leah as she held her and rocked her, her eyes wide as she listened to the sound from above.

Grabbing Kristina, he slipped an arm around Suzi and shoved her over toward the far side of the room, past the bed.

Suzi fell, her knees hitting the rock hard

ground just as the loud roar of the approaching storm cut off all conversation.

They'd made it just in time.

The storm had arrived.

Chapter Fourteen

"Mommy, are you okay?"

Suzi glanced at her daughter whose eyes glowed with fear. She reached out and pulled Kristina into her arms.

They could hear the destruction going on around them. The sounds were so loud they nearly blocked out their own speech.

An arm slipped around Suzi, and the soft, soothing tones of Mitch's voice as he prayed filled her ears. Suzi could feel her daughter trembling. Before she could think of a way to reassure her they would make it out of this, Laura started singing. Leah picked up the tune almost immediately, clinging to Laura as she did. Suzi recognized the song of worship and joined in, clutching Mitch and her daughter even as he clutched her and they continued to pray.

It seemed like an eternity, though Suzi knew storms rarely lasted more than fifteen minutes. Slowly, however, the sound subsided and the only noise heard was the soft worship songs the group sang as the spirit of the Lord came down and surrounded them with His peace.

Finally, Mitch whispered, "I think the worst is over."

"Praise God," Laura whispered.

Quiet reigned, and then Kristina whispered, "Can I go tell my friends about this?"

The suppressed exhilaration in her voice caused them all to chuckle. Leave it to a child to see only the excitement.

"In school," Leah said softly, "you can give a special report and tell everyone how God kept us all safe."

Her gaze met Suzi's, then Mitch's, and Suzi could sense Leah's embarrassment from earlier. She didn't comment, only tried to offer a look of understanding.

"I think, my little angel," Mitch whispered, running a finger up Kristina's tummy, "that I should go out first and check things over. Then, when I see it's safe, we'll all go up, okay?"

He glanced at Laura who nodded. Then he glanced at Suzi.

Only then did Suzi realize she still clung to Mitch and he to her. When she tried to move away, however, she noted his reluctance to release her.

He finally did, but only to arm's length. "Let me check out your mama's injury here first though, sweetie. Laura, do you have a medical kit?"

The small storage compartment in the cellar filled with supplies opened easily. Laura pulled out a kit. Leah took it from her and moved forward.

Suzi was certain it was a peace offering as she held it out to Mitch. He accepted it, not noticing—his gaze trained on Suzi's cheek. With a gentle hand he cupped her chin and tilted her head where he could see something, but there was very little light.

Scowling, he asked, "Can you light the lantern, Laura?"

His thumb stroked across the arch of Suzi's cheek. She flinched as she realized it did indeed hurt there.

The striking of a match could be heard followed shortly by the smell of sulfur and lamp oil which filled the humid air.

Kristina stood closely, watching every movement until Laura turned the radio on, which distracted Kristina from her close inspection. She hopped up and bounded over to help tune in a station.

"I could have lost you today, Suzi-q," Mitch murmured quietly so the others wouldn't overhear.

"I couldn't leave you out there," she argued, protesting just as quietly.

He hesitated, then turned his attention to the kit. Rummaging through it, his large dark hands made the kit look like a kid's toy. He knew what he was looking for, though. He pulled out a clean cloth.

Tearing it open, he treated her cheek,

wiping gently despite his size. Mitch was always like that—gentle. That's why Suzi loved him, and why she'd gone out after him. She'd known there was no way he could hurry Leah along, when Leah had been in a full panic.

"It's going to be swollen back here," he said touching above her ear, "but you only have a small scratch showing."

Pulling out the ointment, he smeared some on his callused fingers so very carefully, the scowl on his face making Leah uneasy, Suzi noted. That was just Mitch. The more worried he was, the more he scowled. She smiled up at him and touched his hand hoping to calm him.

Mitch froze for a moment, then relaxed a bit and turned. Pulling out another package, he returned to inspecting her cheek before gently applying an adhesive patch.

"It's not important," Suzi said, shoving at his hand.

"But it is," he replied, his gaze touching every plane and feature of her face. "It definitely is."

"They say there's another major cell

moving this way,'' Laura interrupted, turning from the radio toward Suzi and Mitch. Suzi wasn't sure if she was happy or aggravated that Laura had broken into the private conversation.

Something was happening, something magical, as they knelt there. She wasn't sure what or how or why, but something was going on. Still, the mood was broken as reality intruded.

Mitch turned. Frowning, he nodded. ''Let me go up and see how bad the damage is and then call in to work. I'll be right back down.''

''I'm going, too,'' Suzi informed him, pushing back to stand.

Mitch shook his head. ''It'd be best if you stayed here with Kristina and Laura and Leah.''

''I want to go.'' She wanted out of the confining space, to go back up and see the branch that had hit her, possibly spend a few minutes alone with Mitch and see if she could figure out what had just happened between them. If it was simply fear, anger, frustration—or something more—Suzi would like to know. Had she imagined the strange look in Mitch's eyes? Was his caress just a bit unsure and different than it had been a year or two ago?

Mitch gave Suzi a resigned look and then sighed.

If she didn't know better, she'd say he was nervous about being alone with her.

Still, he helped Suzi to her feet.

She pushed her hair back again as he strode forward and loosened the rope. Hurrying forward, she was determined that he not leave her behind.

He shoved the door.

It didn't move.

Suzi nearly ran into him when he didn't start right up the stairs. "What is it?"

Mitch shoved again.

"It's stuck?"

She stared as Mitch's muscles bunched again and again as he shoved at the door. There was give on their side from the dark paneling, but on the other side—nothing was happening.

They couldn't be stuck. Doors like this

could not stick. Cement on cement didn't "stick."

Low mutters about the ancestry of the maple tree and then all maple trees in general reached Suzi's hearing. She couldn't help but giggle. "A mesquite?" she questioned.

"Useless trees," he acknowledged. Finally he turned to the women in the cellar. "Well, ladies, it looks like we're not going anywhere. Evidently something has fallen on the cellar and we're blocked in."

A heartbeat of silence ensued before Laura burst out laughing. "I think, Mitch McCade, that this was you and your brother's way of making sure I didn't go in to work!" With another giggle, Laura moved across the cellar to the double bed and as gracefully as possible, she lay down.

Kristina had crawled up next to Laura and had her hand on Laura's tummy while she carried the radio in the other.

Mitch pulled Suzi down next to him on a bench and then stretched out his legs in front of him. Two small windows, one on each side of the cellar, were cracked open;

the small metal plates covering them angled just enough to provide fresh air.

Suzi couldn't help the chuckle that escaped her lips. "I suppose we could be stuck with worse company—like two dozen wet cats."

Ruefully, Mitch shook his head.

"I don't understand." Leah glanced from Mitch to Suzi, then to Laura, before moving over to sit down on a small camping stool against one wall.

Suzi smiled at Leah. "I was over here visiting once when we had a twister scare. The cat that lived out in the barn had just had kittens and I didn't want them to die—"

"She had Zach bring the kittens down here." Mitch muttered.

"How sweet," Leah offered quietly.

Mitch slowly shook his head. "The mama cat, a barn cat, didn't like anyone touching her, let alone her babies. Zach ended up scratched up and the kittens cried all night and smelled like wet mildew."

Leah blinked. "Oh, oh my. I hadn't thought about that."

"And they crawled everywhere. No one got a wink of sleep."

"You sleep down here?" Laura asked.

Mitch glanced at Laura. "You sure didn't have many experiences with tornadoes back in Louisiana did you, Laurie?"

Slowly, she shook her head. "Even if we did, we didn't have cellars."

"Why not?" Leah asked.

"Where are you from?" Laura asked Leah. "Pen...back East," Leah whispered.

Laura nodded. "The water table where I lived was so high they buried people above the ground."

"Oh! Oh, I've seen that on the Information channel. They have entire graveyards built above ground."

Laura chuckled. "Yes, they do."

"We've spent many a night down here, Laura," Suzi cut in. "Just like I have in the town shelter or at a neighbor's. If you have a long string of thunderstorms that are touching off twisters, you don't want to go up and sleep until the 'all clear' is given. A lot of times, Mom would just tuck me in at a neighbor's house and we'd stay all night.''

Mitch broke in. "Zach usually kept us down here, too. Our mom and dad used to insist, whenever there was a tornado, that we had to stay down here and that it was easier, with three kids, just to stay the night.''

"This is the first bad storm I've been in since marrying Zach," Laura mused now.

"I've never experienced this," Leah added.

Kristina, Suzi noted, was sound asleep, radio clutched in one hand, and her other one on Laura's tummy.

"I've been in several," Suzi said absently.

Mitch reached out and nudged Suzi. "You might as well rest. It sounds like another storm is moving in and we're going to be here awhile. What time was my brother due back?" he asked, directing his question toward Laura.

Suzi allowed Mitch to adjust her until she was leaning back against him on the large padded bench.

"He and Angela were flying back tonight around eight."

"I wonder if Julian will think to send someone out this way."

"Your work?" Leah asked.

Mitch shook his head. "I told them I was staying out here with Suzi and Laura. They won't think a thing if I don't call in. They'll simply imagine I'm out here helping."

"I hope the horses are okay. And all the work on Zach's office…"

Reality was slowly setting in. Mitch worked to soothe Laura. "Don't worry, Laura. Just dwell on the fact we're all safe. I think that'll mean more to Zach than a new office would."

"Besides, we don't know that it's not there," Suzi added.

"That's right," Leah echoed, working to sound cheerful.

"What made you come out here?" Suzi asked now.

"We were on our way out when we heard the weather reports and I thought it'd be safer to find cover so we continued on."

"You were right, Leah," Mitch said.

The question hovering, unasked, hummed in the air. Why had Leah panicked and run from Mitch? Why had she fought him until Suzi had finally slapped her?

Instead of asking the question, everyone politely ignored that it had happened. They retold tales, passed down from mothers and fathers to children, of other disasters or accidents that had happened to them, doing the ritual storytelling of past emergencies as the time passed—seven, and then eight o'clock.

Mitch broke out food and fed a bouncy Kristina, doling out supplies to the women in the cellar.

He wondered how long it would take for Zach to find them. It was after 8 p.m. and they weren't home yet. Mitch wondered if the airport was still operating or if the weather had stopped the flights. It wasn't surprising, with farms so widespread, that no one had checked out here yet. Was the Native American reservation okay, he had to wonder? And Julian's in-laws. How had they fared?

There was no one to answer the questions, so instead of posing them, he worked to stay nonchalant and listen to Suzi answer Laura's questions about childbirth.

"Messy? No, not really. She was born easily enough. After hours and hours of labor."

"Zach said you almost lost her."

Mitch heard that and glanced at Suzi in query. Kristina had finally, exhausted, dropped back into a sleep. Laura sat propped up against the headboard made from two-by-fours. The oil lamp cast a dim light on the occupants of the small, square, cement cell.

Suzi shook her head. "It was hard, but God is faithful. My baby was born fine."

An odd note in Suzi's voice had Mitch wondering just what she wasn't saying. How long had he known her, but not seen these small things? Or perhaps, he'd been so concerned about his own future that he just hadn't caught the nuances in her voice.

He'd always thought he'd known her as well as himself. In some ways he had, but he was finding, just in the last few hours, that an entire new world had opened up to him—one he'd never seen before.

One through the eyes of love.

Mitch froze.

Love?

Oh, no. Not him. Not Suzi. Not the *two* of them. *Together.*

"Mitch?"

"Huh?" For a moment he'd completely forgotten he still held Suzi in his arms. The sound of Suzi's voice right after that dumbfounding revelation nearly made him drop her. It took every bit of willpower not to jump and run. Of course, where could he run? Five feet away? In a room full of women who would each have their own questions as to why he was acting like a chicken without any brains?

"We're almost out of oil for the lamp. Did you get any extra before we came down?" Laura broke in.

Mitch glanced at the lamp and saw the low, flickering flame. He could hear the storm picking up for the countless number of times tonight and sighed, "I'm sorry, Laura. That, I didn't think of."

His gaze dropped down to the woman sitting next to him. "I guess we'll just have to kill the lamp and wait until Zach and Angie get here, Laura."

Suzi started to get up.

"I'll get it," Leah said, and hurried over to the lamp. Carefully, she reached up and cupped her hand around the top of the glass globe and then, with a puff, their cement sanctuary was plunged into darkness.

The only light was the flashes of lightning outside that would light up sections of the cellar just enough to show the five shadows resting, waiting for rescue.

"I'm sure it won't be long now," Laura murmured.

Mitch heard her adjust.

"Leah, come on over and share the bed. It's going to be a long night."

There was movement and then the sound of the creaking ropes of the bed. Mitch didn't say anything as he was still trying to come to terms with what he'd just realized.

He was in love with his best friend.

How could he see her as a future lover

and wife though, instead of a friend who—who what?

Shifting, she refitted herself against him and his arms automatically went back around her, repositioning her to rest comfortably.

Who had what? he asked himself again.

Who had always been there? She'd been there when he'd gotten his first black eye—the one she'd given him—and she'd been there when he had lost his first girlfriend to Noble. When his parents had died she'd been there. As a matter of fact, she had always been there for him.

They went out to eat together, talked, laughed, shared everything.

Like friends were suppose to do.

But lovers? Husband and wife? Joined together under God's sight?

Trying to imagine what it would be like when he married and moved on and Suzi no longer had a special place in his life, he found he couldn't even conceive that.

"You're squeezing me, Mitch." Suzi's gasping voice wheezed out near his chest.

Mitch immediately loosened his hold,

which he realized had actually been crushing in its embrace.

"Are you okay?" that same voice whispered. Her hand came up and touched his other shoulder as she adjusted and tried to look up through the darkness at him to gauge his mood. Suzi was always doing that—looking him in the eyes as if she could see what he thought.

Mitch nodded, then added, "Yeah." It was dark. She couldn't see him. A small measure of relief touched him at that thought. At least she wouldn't see the utter shock on his face as he tried to come to grips with his discovery. He worked to bring his roiling emotions under control.

"Rest then. It'll be a while before we get out." Her sleepy voice whispered the last on a sigh.

Mitch thought she might get some rest, but after his revelation tonight, he wasn't sure he was ever going to get another day's rest, not for the rest of his life.

Chapter Fifteen

"Well, Sheriff, looks like we've about got things tied up here. What do you think?" Mitch glanced over at his deputy and nodded. "It's been a long three days."

Standing, he stretched, rotating his shoulder muscles to ease the ache.

"I want to thank you again for getting Laura down into the cellar like that." The young man's grateful voice reminded Mitch again of the dangers Laura and many others had faced only three days before.

Mitch tucked in his shirt and nodded. "No problem, Mark. Glad you were okay."

Turning to face Laura's brother he

grinned. "I wish you could have seen Zach's face when he finally got to us. After his initial shock, his first words were, he'd come to the office expecting to find Laura working. Then with his humor kicking in, he'd made a comment about her staying at the ranch because she was more worried about that ornery horse of hers, Jingle Bells."

Mark finished filling up a small leather bag on his desk. Mitch watched how carefully he repacked his camera and other tools as they talked. "Yeah," he said, humor kicking up the corners of his own mouth, "my sister isn't going to let you live that down."

Mitch chuckled. "I imagine she won't." When Mark swung the pack up to his shoulder, Mitch changed the subject. "I promised Zach and Laura I'd be out to dinner tonight. You going to be there?"

Even though Mark was only three years younger than his sister Laura, he was taller, thin and athletic in looks. He did all the photography for the sheriff's department and as well as acting as a deputy sheriff.

But now, faced with that simple question he ran a hand through his dark hair and with a rueful smile he said, "Listen to another lecture by my big sister about being out during the storm? I don't think so."

Mitch chuckled. Laura certainly did run roughshod over Mark sometimes. The storm was one of those instances and Mark was determined to stay in hiding until his sister calmed down. "Well, then, I appreciate your help. I think we have all the areas that were hit photographed and on video." He sighed, thinking again of the mess.

"It could have been worse. Had this been a large community, it would have been devastating." Mark moved around his desk and straightened the last of the work folders lying there to tuck away.

"Yeah. Well, Mrs. Culpepper lost her barn and several of our farms lost livestock and line shacks."

"You were lucky that Zach only lost one of the big maples, the old barn and part of his fence. It'll only take a month or two to complete the repairs. His livestock loss was minimal.'' Mark carried most of those folders to the dispatcher for later filing.

"I know. At least it missed most of the town. Oh, did you get the pictures of the roof at the general store for our records?''

"Sure did.'' Mark moved back over to his desk and riffled through the other folders before holding up one.

"Great.''

"Boss, will you stop worrying and go on home? You've spent nearly the last three days in this office.'' Dana, the new dispatcher called from her desk. Her curly red hair bounced as she waved for him to leave.

Mitch knew he should, but it wasn't only the storm and work on his mind.

If only it were that easy.

No, Suzi filled his thoughts as well.

When Zach had rescued them the other night, things had been hectic. They'd gone up, seen the devastation and set immediately to work checking on horses, livestock and such. Mitch, afraid Zach would see something Mitch didn't want him to see, had insisted on going in to work as soon as possible.

That was the last time he'd seen Suzi.

She had been standing near the cellar door, holding Kristina, watching him drive off.

The more time that had passed, the less he'd wanted to talk to her. The less he'd known *how* to talk to her. The last three days had been spent working or catnapping on a cot in his office as he and his office staff had worked to make sure everything was taken care of after the nasty twister that had cut a swath through several ranching areas of Hill Creek.

But now...

It was time to face Suzi. If he avoided her any more, she'd wonder why. He just wasn't sure how he was going to tell her how he felt. How did one go about telling his best friend that he wasn't looking at her like a best friend but...?

"Boss?"

Mitch glanced over at the dispatcher. "Yeah?"

"I asked if you wanted us to give you a wake-up call if anything major happens."

"Oh." Mitch nodded. Stretching, he

turned, grabbed his jacket and headed toward the door. "Do that. I'll have my radio or pager nearby. Just code in what you need."

With a check of his belt to make sure he still had his pager, he left the office.

Slipping his jacket on, he started down the street. It was still early, though school had already started. He could hear the kids nearby on the playground. He had several hours yet before he had to be at the ranch for dinner tonight.

If he was going to talk to Suzi, it might as well be now. The clouded skies and the wind kicking up provided relief from the hot summer days.

They'd probably have some more rain. Mitch knew the ranchers would appreciate that. Rain would be good right now because later in the year they wouldn't be getting much. Except the saturated ground made them a prime candidate for flash floods.

Luckily, not too many places had to worry about flash floods out here. Just some rural areas.

Straightening his hat, he pointed himself

in the direction of Suzi's and decided to walk.

Maybe he was walking simply to take a bit longer. Then again, he did want to look over several areas in town one more time and stop by the store for a treat to leave for Kristina and...

Stopping, he propped his hands on his hips and tipped his head up to stare at the clouded sky. "It's easy, Mitch. You go up to her and say 'Suzi, we have to talk. I have to be married by July 4th. Would you consider being my wife?' Then hope she doesn't laugh at you."

Shaking his head in disgust, he turned and strode back toward his vehicle. "No reason putting it off. If you have time to think, you'll come up with something worse than that," he muttered to himself.

Pulling out his keys, he put everything else from his mind, including approaching Suzi about that and the fact that July 4th was only two weeks away. He would simply talk to her. July 4th. He'd been crazy to set down a stupid date like that. Who cared if he married by the fourth or not?

Climbing into his vehicle he started it and headed down the street to Suzi's.

As he pulled up, he examined the house Suzi lived in. There was no damage to her house, thankfully. If anything, the high winds and rain had peeled more paint away.

He wouldn't mind painting the house for her, or anything else she needed. He'd just tell her he lost the bet. Yeah, that was it. He'd tell her he decided it didn't matter that he wanted more out of marriage and then start painting her house.

Mitch felt the huge knot of worry leave. It was the perfect excuse. And while he was painting her house, he could court her and eventually make his plans known to her— that he loved her.

"You're crazy, Mitch," he muttered.

Still, it was better than asking her right out to marry him. Turning off the engine he shoved open the truck door and walked up to her house. With a deep breath he pushed the doorbell.

It echoed inside.

Mitch waited.

When Suzi didn't answer, he rang the

bell again, then knocked. "Suzi?" he called out and reached for the door.

He'd tell her that he was concerned about her losing her job, he decided, as he turned the handle to the door.

That would be perfect. She'd lost her job and needed someone to take care of her. And he wanted kids and knew she'd make a good mother....

The door was locked.

Frowning, he twisted it to make sure.

Stepping back he looked at the door. Suzi never locked her door when she was home.

Glancing over to the side of the house he realized her car wasn't here.

With a sigh, Mitch realized he wasn't going to be telling her anything because Suzi wasn't home.

Suzi wasn't home.

He thought about that a moment.

Where would she be this time of the morning?

Shopping?

At school?

Mitch shook his head. Turning, he started back toward his truck. His radio crackled.

Mitch picked it up as he climbed into his vehicle. "What is it?"

"Your sister-in-law Laura is over at the hospital and wondered if you could stop by."

Mitch's mind was diverted briefly. "Is it the baby?"

"I don't know, Sheriff. She didn't say."

"Tell her I'm on my way."

Starting his engine, he headed over there, deciding it would be a good way to waste some time until Suzi got back home.

He didn't even have to get out of the vehicle. As he drove up, he saw Laura outside waiting for him. She waddled over and pulled open the door. "I was wondering if you could give me a ride to your office, Mitch."

Mitch held out a hand and assisted her up into his vehicle.

"What are you doing in town, honey?" he asked as Laura worked to adjust her big bulk around in the car.

"Oh, I had an appointment. They were going to do an ultrasound but the technician didn't show up today. I was tired of waiting. Zach dropped me off, but won't be back into town until later and Freckles is out making rounds to some of the clinic people."

"And Hawk?"

"Special medical class in Dallas. Gone for the next three days. Drumming up federal money or some such. I thought, if you didn't mind, I'd wait at your office."

Mitch shook his head. "I'll take you home, Laura. I'm done for the day."

"Are you sure?" she asked, and shifted again as she worked to get the seatbelt adjusted the way she wanted it.

"Sure am."

Smiling, she shoved the hair out of her face. "I am absolutely miserable. If I get any bigger I swear..." she declared, drifting off, and with a huff fell back against the seat. "I am so absolutely exhausted from waiting, Mitch."

Mitch turned his four-by-four toward the ranch and headed out of town. "I bet you are, Laura. So, what was so important for Zach that he just dropped you off today?"

Laura grinned. "He's picking up the

horse the man was supposed to deliver. I decided just to tell Zach and let him go get it. The man is too busy with repairs to his own ranch to do any delivering right now.''

''And what did my brother say about his gift?'' Mitch asked, as he hit the highway and passed out of the city limits.

Laura grinned one of her secret grins. ''He was very pleased.'' Then she chuckled, ''Except he realized it meant I'd been out around the horses again.''

Mitch chuckled too.

He heard her shift again before she asked, ''And how are you doing?''

''Just fine. A bit tired.''

''Oh. That's good. I'm so glad to hear that.''

Mitch's smile faded at the tone in her voice. ''Why wouldn't I be doing okay, Laura?''

The land stretched out for miles, few trees dotting the landscape. Cacti and prairie grass, along with barbed-wire fences held by wooden poles, added to the dark desolate picture that only a person from the area could appreciate.

Dark gray skies hung low with the promise of soon-to-come rain.

However, for some reason, Laura's tone made him feel that a thunderstorm was about to break out right there in his four-by-four.

"Oh, I thought you knew. Um, Mitch, maybe we should—"

"Laura?" Mitch asked, alarm slowly raising its unwanted head and working its way up to be foremost in his thoughts. "What is it?"

"Oh, Mitch. Look. It's nothing that big, really. I just thought you would have known about Suzi—I mean…"

Panic hit his gut. "What about her?" he demanded, casting a harsh look her way.

Her eyes widened in distress. "Okay, boss," she said, falling back on her nickname for him. "Please don't get upset. We didn't mention anything when you called yesterday because we were giving you time…it's just…"

"Your hesitation is what is alarming me, deputy," he said shortly to Laura. "Just tell me!"

Laura rolled her eyes. "I swear, Mitch McCade, you can be as bad tempered as your brother. Okay, okay. She's working for Bate Masterson."

Mitch felt the storm inside him explode just as the skies opened up and began to pour their own fury.

Chapter Sixteen

"I'll kill him."

"Mitch McCade!" Laura said in shock. "You repent of that right now. I don't want to hear that out of your mouth again."

Mitch flinched at the harshness in Laura's voice. She was right, though. "He probably coerced her," Mitch muttered.

"What makes you say that?"

Mitch didn't continue but turned on the mile road and headed out toward Bate's house.

"Mitch?"

"You stay in the car when we get there. I'm just going to talk to her."

"You are not going out to Mr. Masterson's ranch. You're too emotionally involved in this. I won't let you go up there alone," she warned.

Mitch growled.

Laura chuckled. "There's a sound I recognize. You sound just like Zach when you do that."

He scowled. "Women."

"All women? Or just those who don't obey your orders?" Laura asked mildly. "This seat feels like it's filled with rocks," she muttered and shifted again. "Every time I think I'm comfortable…"

"Tell me, why would Suzi go to work for a piece of…?"

"I know, Mitch," Laura said into the silence. "You don't think he's changed at all?"

Mitch sighed. Reviewing the latest gossip he'd heard, he finally shook his head. "I don't think so. I hadn't mentioned anything to Suzi, but one of my deputies said they've got some information that there's action again."

"Oh, no."

"Exactly. Over on the county line. It's only a rumor, but it started up shortly after Noble got back."

"What makes him do that?"

Mitch shrugged. "I don't know. What makes anyone do what they do?"

"Yeah," Laura said. Then she added softly, "What makes people like us look back at our past, try to correct it, never give up and just look forward?"

Mitch's gaze shifted briefly to Laura. There was understanding in her eyes. "I wanted to please my father. Even though he was dead, I had to prove to him that I could be what I wanted to be, the best cop on the force back in Louisiana."

Mitch didn't like where this conversation was going. "Your point?" he asked.

Laura wiggled, then sighed. "It's obvious, Mitch. Your whole family has allowed their anger toward the Mastersons to eat at them. Zach and Hawk have released most of that and given it to God. Don't think about your parents, about what they've done or didn't do. It's not your fault they took off on that trip, and well, okay, maybe they were angry and about to enter into a court battle with Bate Masterson before they took off on that trip. But that was the past. Sooner or later you're going to have to let it go."

"Why are you bringing this up now?" Mitch asked, gripping the wheel in the torrential downpour. He slowed as they came to the creek crossing that separated his land from Masterson's land.

"Because you're headed out to Mr. Masterson's house right now. And before you go chasing down Suzi, you'd better ask yourself just how much you hate them and just how much you love her."

"What is that supposed to mean?" Mitch had no idea what she was talking about.

"That water is coming up quick," Laura murmured quietly.

Mitch noted it was already to the doors. What was he doing going through water that deep?

Shaking his head he said, "Man, Laura. I shouldn't have gone through that. We're going to have to take the long way home to avoid this. It's going to be too swollen to cross on the way back."

"You're not thinking clearly, Mitch."

"Yeah," he finally conceded, frustration rife in his voice. "But how could she go to work for him? Bate caused so many problems for our family it isn't even funny."

"You don't think you're seeing Bate reaping the results now? Come on, Mitch," Laura argued, "wake up. The law nailed his son for his involvement in a drug ring. Yeah, he got off, but he's under investigation, they've already ceased production on over thirty percent of Bate's land, and they're investigating his records. The man is not the arrogant mega-power he used to be out here. Have you actually looked at him lately?"

"He's the enemy!" Mitch said harshly.

"No. He's the *tool* the enemy used! Not only to get at you but to get you to waste energy on hatred!"

Mitch blinked. He'd never heard Laura yell before. Turning, he stared at her briefly.

Her gaze was dead serious. "And I'm

just supposed to forgive and forget?'' he asked now.

"Jesus did."

Mitch flushed red with anger. "I'm not Him."

"Thank goodness for small favors."

He felt guilt and conviction tearing at him. "Suzi had no business going to work for these people."

"She needed a job."

"I could've found her a job at the office," Mitch growled.

"She doesn't want a job from you, Mitch."

"What else am I supposed to do? Huh? You have all the answers suddenly, Laura. Tell me. You think I should just leave her here and ignore her? I shouldn't go out here and get her? I should let her work with someone who is surely back into his old business?"

Laura smiled. "I think you should tell her you love her and then there'd be no question as to whether she stayed out here or not."

"What are you talking about?"

"Oh, look. Here's the ranch," Laura said sweetly.

"Women," Mitch muttered again. "I don't know how Zach puts up with you."

"Same way you do. You know I'm right."

"Okay. Okay, enough. I promise you, Laura, I won't punch out Bate Masterson and I'll do my best to be polite and really look at him this time."

"And you'll tell Suzi you love her?"

"I'll *consider* telling Suzi. I may have my own timing for that, if you don't mind."

Mitch thanked God when the woman didn't say anything else. However, as he thought about it, he realized he wasn't near as angry as when he'd first started out this way.

Laura had effectively diffused his anger.

Pulling up in front of the house, he shoved the truck into park and hopped out. "I'll be right back, Laura."

"Please don't argue with her. Give her a chance to explain."

Mitch nodded, and then, repositioning his

hat, he hurried up the steps of the sprawling three-story ranch house.

At the top of the steps, he strode forward and rang the bell. A maid opened the door almost immediately.

"I need to speak with Suzi…"

"McCade."

Forcing himself not to stiffen, Mitch turned to confront the voice coming from the hallway. He turned to confront Bate Masterson.

Tall, boisterous, a man of steel was how Mitch had always thought of him. However, staring at him now, Mitch noted age lines around his eyes and a bit more of a stoop to his shoulders he'd never noticed before. The man was still a formidable person, but maybe just not quite as impenetrable as he'd thought.

Mitch took off his hat. "Afternoon, Mr. Masterson. I stopped by to see Suzi."

Masterson paused, his brow furrowing. "Ah, yes. Nice little thing. Came out to apply for a job two days ago. I needed help and took her right in."

Cynically, Mitch started to say something

about how innocent Bate sounded. However, simple manners and Laura's warning kept him from being nasty to this older man.

"She lost her job at the school."

Absently, Bate nodded.

It was then Mitch noted all the papers the man held in his hand.

"I—well, you can go find her," he said and turned, heading off down the hall.

Just like that, he was gone.

Mitch glanced back at the timid young woman who had answered the door. "She's in the housekeeper's office," she whispered and pointed. "Go down that hall, turn right and then you'll go back left. Last room on the left. Would you like me to show you?"

Mitch shook his head. "I think I can find it. Thank you, *señorita*." With a gentle smile he headed down the hall.

He was right. He found it easily. Slowing in front of the door, he saw Suzi sitting and riffling through a pile of papers. She looked beautiful today in her jeans and pink ruffled collar top that buttoned down the front, and her long, dark hair pulled back and piled up on her head.

Her brow furrowed in concentration.

He opened his mouth to say something— but found himself speechless.

When she sat back to stretch, she saw him. How long had he been standing there staring at her? "Mitch?"

"Can I come in?"

She only nodded.

Mitch walked in and crossed to a chair that angled toward the desk. It was nice furniture, he had to give Bate that. Padded chairs, a comfortable couch, tea served in a carafe.

"I was going to tell you."

Disbelief flashed in Mitch's eyes. "Oh. When, Suzi?"

"You've been busy."

"You could have called me."

"Or you me."

Suzi sighed. Running a hand over her forehead she said, "Okay, let's talk. What happened, Mitch? Why did you run like that?"

Mitch shifted in his chair. "I didn't run, Suzi."

Suzi glanced up at him. Lifting an eyebrow in disbelief she said, "Oh? How long have I known you, Mitch McCade? How long have we been best friends? Don't tell me that wasn't a full retreat."

Scowling, he said, "And you haven't been in retreat yourself? I told you I wanted to get you a cell phone before you came out here. I wanted you to have something just in case you needed me. You knew that, but you didn't even call me."

He was right. Suzi knew it and so did he. She did take the job on the sly, so to speak. She had wanted to avoid a blowup with Mitch.

She didn't like the Mastersons all that much, but Bate had been totally professional. And it was true, he did need someone to manage the accounts and housekeeping staff. At least Noble hadn't been lying about that.

"I wanted the job," she said now.

And it was true. At first she hadn't, but now…the pay was wonderful, and Bate was completely understanding about her having a child. She had been flabbergasted when she'd realized Bate knew nothing about her daughter. She wasn't sure what game Noble was playing, but at least the job was legit.

"Why?"

Shrugging at the blunt question, she answered. "It's challenging. I'll admit when Noble came to me I didn't believe him. But I don't think I have to work around him at all. At least, I haven't seen him that much since I came out here. I'm doing household accounts, handling staff. It's far more than I could have hoped for without a degree."

"Suzi..."

"Mitch, I'm sorry, but you have to understand."

"Understand what?"

Shaking her head, she sighed. "I know how you feel about this family, but what does it matter to you? You're looking to get married to someone like Leah or one of a dozen other women and I have to look after a future for my daughter. This is a good job. I have to give it a try."

"Not if you marry me."

"So you see—what?"

Mitch shrugged, his features inscrutable. "I vowed to marry by the Fourth. The time is nearly here. Why not marry. We're best friends. I can provide for you and Kristina."

"I—I—I—" This was what she'd hoped for, but for the life of her, she couldn't form a coherent word. How many years had she wanted to marry him, dreamed of marrying and settling down with this very man? She'd always imagined him getting down on one knee and proclaiming his love, or maybe while at a movie or on a drive.

But here, in the Mastersons' house?

"You just want me out of here."

"Of course I do, Suzi. I don't want you working here. But there's more. Why don't you come with me and we'll talk about it."

"But—"

"Come on…"

"I have to work." What could she say? This wasn't *her* Mitch. "Mitch—I—I don't know what to say. I…"

Mitch glanced down at his boots, turning his hat in his hands. "Suzi, do you have to argue with everything I say? Okay, I love you. It's taken awhile for me to realize it, but—"

"Stop!"

Mitch glanced down at her in surprise.

"Please, don't say another word. I have to talk to you first."

At the confused look on his face, she held up a hand. "Come on, let's go. I'll take a short time to talk with you and then we'll go from there."

Standing, she shot around her desk and toward the door. She only paused long enough to grab Mitch's hand.

His hand was so warm next to her icy one. Oh, how could he spring this on her now?

Loved her? How could he love her? Here? Now?

Couldn't he have waited until tonight to tell her? Oh, what was she thinking...?

"Suzi? Why don't you tell me what's going on?"

Suzi looked to find a passing servant. "Glenda? Tell Mr. Masterson a minor emergency came up and I'll be right back."

"Yes, *señorita*," Glenda replied.

"What would that be?"

Suzi nearly tripped over the thick rug at that voice. She turned white to see Noble coming down the hall from the kitchen. And the gleam in his eyes said he was ready for battle.

Mitch curled his lip in disgust. "Masterson."

"McCade."

"Come on, Mitch," Suzi urged tugging on his rock-hard arm to encourage him down the hall.

"You're still on duty, Suzi," Noble said, smiling slightly.

"I'm sure your father will—"

"I won't," Noble broke in.

"You really think I'll let her work for you, Noble?" Mitch asked quietly. "After the way you treated Julian and his wife?"

"I don't see where you have much say," Noble drawled, the coffee cup in his hand steady, as he rested a shoulder against the wall. "It's her choice."

"Mitch, please," Suzi said.

Glenda wisely chose that moment to slip away from the group.

"She's going to marry me."

Noble spilled his coffee. It wasn't much, but he'd just tipped it to take a sip. Suzi saw it. She was certain Mitch saw it, too, when he nodded shortly and started off.

"I guess we'll be related, sorta then, won't we Sheriff?"

Suzi, who had just started after Mitch stumbled, falling into him when he stopped so suddenly.

"I can't see that," Mitch bit out.

He turned, his gaze filled with loathing as he eyed Noble.

"Oh, it's possible all right."

Suzi thought she was going to be sick. After everything that had just happened, she had planned to tell Mitch as soon as they got out of earshot of the house.

"Suzi?" Mitch's gaze shot to her. She could see he still didn't understand.

"Mitch," she whispered.

"Ask her who comforted her the night you blew out of town."

Mitch understood now. He paled under

his tanned skin. The look of appalled distaste nearly made Suzi cry. Please, God. Oh please, she prayed silently.

"Mitch..."

"Kristina is *his* child?" Mitch demanded.

"My child, all right," Noble confirmed.

"A grandchild!"

Suzi heard the shout and saw Bate Masterson standing in a doorway just behind Mitch.

"You and him?" Mitch said, his voice forcing its way out through a knot of anger. Suzi could tell it from the look on his face.

"Congratulations, Daddy," Noble called out and toasted him.

"Why, Suzi? Why?"

Oh, God, help me, Suzi silently cried.

"Someone congratulate me," a new voice added. "My water just broke and the baby is on the way."

Everyone turned to find Laura McCade standing at the end of the hallway, soaked, looking like she was madder than a wet hen.

Suzi couldn't help it. It was all too much.

Without waiting, she turned and dashed off down the hall, hoping only to get away before the rest of what little world that was left fell out from under her.

Without warning, she turned and dashed off down the hall, hoping only to get away before the rest of what little world that was left fell out from under her.

Chapter Seventeen

"Suzi!"

Mitch hesitated between her and Laura.

"Go," Bate said, his voice full of command as he went over to Laura. "I'll see to this little lady, you can come back when you've settled things."

"I'll be glad to go see after her, McCade," Noble began.

"Shut up or get out, Noble."

The sharp words from Bate to Noble froze everyone except Mitch, who took off after Suzi.

"What?" Noble paused, looking at his father.

"I said shut up or get out. You've caused enough problems. For more than just the McCades. You have a daughter!"

Noble's gaze turned dark. "You're taking *their* side? After everything they've done? Think of what they've cost us," Noble screamed, his anger turning to fury. "They have cost us nearly everything. At one time we owned most of the land here. If McCade's dad had tried a little harder, you wouldn't have gone in on that gamble and lost all you did. You deserve to have everything they have, not just some. And you'll get it all back."

Bate, looking very old at that moment, shook his head. "It's not worth losing your soul, son."

"Son?" Scornfully, Noble laughed. "Like father, like son. How do you like it? I've turned out just like you, Dad. I was only doing it for us."

Bate's gaze narrowed. "I never did what you did. I raised you in church, Noble. I thought I'd instilled something in you. You have a child and haven't even acknowledged her or supported her."

"You instilled hate in him," Laura finally broke in, a bit breathless. "Hate for the McCades."

"I'm going to get what belongs to us," Noble sneered at Laura. With that he pushed past them and strode out the front door.

Laura looked up at Bate who shook his head. "God forgive me, for I never realized until today how eaten-up with hate I was. And it may have cost my son his soul. Come on, young lady, let's get you upstairs and I'll call in some help."

"River's flooded," Laura said, gritting her teeth as a hard contraction hit.

"I bet it is. We'll see what we can arrange."

Taking her by the elbow, he started up the stairs, snapping out orders like a general in a room full of recruits.

At the moment, Laura didn't care who it was, she was only grateful to have someone to take charge.

"Suzi!" Mitch ran out into the rain, after her.

She didn't stop. She put on the speed.

"Suzi!" Mitch shouted, and ran after her. She made it all the way to the barn and was jerking open a horse's stall when Mitch caught up to her.

The smell of pungent hay and horses surrounded her. Men came running from several different directions when they heard the disturbance around the horses.

Mitch waved them off. "Stay out. Get out," he ordered.

Suzi looked over her shoulder, saw him coming and started leading one of the horses out of the stall.

"Stop it, Suzi!" His heart thundered. He saw the tears on her cheeks, the look of shame and fear and hurt that covered her face as she sobbed.

"Just go away, Mitch. Go away!"

Lifting a hand, he motioned to her. "Just stay right there..."

She swung up onto the bare back of the horse and headed, at breakneck speed, out into the rain. "Now, how did I know she would do that?" Mitch growled.

Grabbing another horse, one he knew

was Bate's and well trained, he swung up on the back of the horse and took off after Suzi.

"Hey!" one of the men yelled.

"Sheriff's emergency," he called out, having no idea if the law would protect him or not from grand theft horse.

But he wasn't letting Suzi ride out in this storm alone. "And I only thought these things happened to Zach and Julian," he muttered, and urged the horse onward.

Suzi sailed over a fence. Mitch's heart nearly stopped. "Suzi!" he cried out.

Going around through the gate he continued after her. She reached the wooded area and slowed down.

Mitch was thankful she was at least thinking about that. Shortly, he got to where she had entered the woods. He could hear little over the sound of water in the distance.

Surely she wouldn't try to cross the creek. Urging his horse as fast as possible he followed her trail and caught up to her— at the river.

Dismounted, she knelt about thirty feet from the horse, her head bowed, sobbing.

Mitch quickly tied his horse. Going over, he touched her shoulder.

"No. Mitch, please just go."

This wasn't his Suzi. This was the Suzi who at seventeen had made a mistake and ended up pregnant. This was the Suzi who had "turned to Noble for comfort" according to Noble, when Mitch had run from town in his bad-boy days. This was the scared, lonely, shamed young girl.

Dropping to his knees next to her he pulled her into his arms. "Not this time, Suzi-q. I'm not leaving you this time—or ever again."

"But what he said is true. We were together that one night."

Her tears were tearing his heart out. "Why, Suzi?" he whispered. "Why?"

The deep gut-wrenching sobs shook her body and were easily discernible over the noise around them. "Be—be—because I—I—I wanted you and you weren't there and I decided…"

She burst into sobs again and Mitch held her close. He felt his own tears start as he knew what was coming. He knew his Suzi. "So, you thought, to show me how angry you were, how angry you were not only at me, but also at God, you'd do the worst possible thing you could think to do?"

She nodded against his chest. "It was the only thing I could think of..."

And it had haunted her ever since that night.

Pulling her tight against him, he rubbed his hands up and down her back.

"I'm so sorry, Mitch. I don't know what I was thinking. But when you left—saying you were never coming back—I've always loved you and..."

"It was my fault, Suzi," Mitch whispered. "My hatred of one family warped you in a small way, too."

"Sin is awful," Suzi whispered now, between her dying sobs. "Six years now I've lived in fear of the truth."

"Sin is awful," he acknowledged. "My hatred reached out, touched you..."

Suzi shuddered and another sob escaped. "I'm sorry, Mitch. I just—I wanted you to fall for me like I had you. It's so stupid, looking back at it, but at the time—"

"But I do love you, Suzi. I've stayed around because you needed me. I couldn't desert my best friend."

"Best friends," she whispered.

"Well..." Mitch hesitated.

Her arms squeezed him. "It's not important. I'm just sorry you found out the way you did, Mitch."

"What? That you love me?"

Suzi stilled. Looking up at him, she shook her head. His words stunned her. It showed in her gaze. "No, that I...I...you know...with Noble."

Mitch took a deep breath. "I've allowed hate to guide me enough. Hate, and the fact that I was trying to prove something to someone in my past. Suzi-q, all I want now is you."

"Me? But—"

"But what?" he asked, and cupped her cheek, wiping at the water on her face.

"But I...sinned."

Mitch couldn't help chuckling. "We all have, Suzi. Kristina wasn't an immaculate conception. But you said it was under the blood. Jesus forgave you and washed it away. Because of that who am I to ever question you on it?"

"It doesn't bother you?"

Mitch had to be honest. "For a split second it did. I felt—betrayed, angry and furious. But Suzi, I felt hurt too. Hurt that you would go to him and hurt that I had left and allowed it to happen."

"You don't control me."

"No, but I think I've always loved you."

Suzi gaped.

Mitch leaned forward and very carefully covered her lips with his own. They were so soft, trembling with all of the emotion slipping out over the terrible secret that had just been revealed in such a shocking way.

Mitch didn't mind. He waited and then gently, ever so gently, with all of the love he felt in his heart, he caressed her lips with his.

Kneeling there, together in the mud, the rain, the smell of pine and the sound of rushing water, Mitch finally admitted that this was his future, this love, and this unity that he had found sent from God. Suzi was his future. Now, to get back to delivering a baby…

Epilogue

Suzi stood nervously, her hands clasped in front of her as Freckles and Laura played with her dress. "Are you sure I look okay?"

Laura grinned. "Better than I do!" She poked at her still flabby tummy.

"How is Zach adjusting to a new baby?" Freckles asked reaching down and pulling at the empire lace-covered waist of Suzi's dress.

Laura grinned. "He and Angela fight over who gets to hold Alexander Phillip first."

"How did Mitch look?" Suzi asked.

Laura smiled. "With Bate sitting in the front row on your side?" A giggle escaped.

"He's proud of his granddaughter."

"Now there is a man who has really changed," Freckles said, and moved around to the train. "Kristina, come help me with Mama's train. Look at this, it has red rug pieces on it. Help me pick them off."

"*¿Qué?*" Suzi cried and tried to see.

"It's okay. Just from the new carpet put down in the church after the tornado."

"Hey, Freckles, there's our music. Come on, Kristina. Let's go. Grab your flowers."

"You know," Freckles said, moving up behind Laura. "I've been watching Leah and your brother and I wondered—"

"Nah. My brother would never consider—"

"Will you two stop it? We have a wedding here!"

Both women looked around at Suzi, sympathetic gazes on their faces.

"Do you think she's handling this better than Mitch?"

In unison, they said, "No!"

Suzi rolled her eyes. "Go, there is your cue."

Laura started out in her bright red, flowing gown.

She had to wonder how Mitch was handling this. After Bate had delivered the baby two weeks ago when no doctor had come in time to help, things had drastically changed. Julian, Freckles and Zach had made it over about an hour after the child had been born. Mitch had assisted in the delivery.

Noble was gone. No one was sure where. They could see the pain in Bate's gaze, but, since he'd made enough of a mess of their lives, he said he had to leave it in God's hands. He was praying for a miracle.

And amazingly enough, so were Zach, Mitch and Hawk. Their families were healing. Mitch had sort of turned green when he found out Suzi had offered to let Bate sit on her side of the pew if he wanted, since he was related. She had vowed no more secrets.

"Your turn, Freckles," Suzi whispered, her anxiousness building. "Hurry."

"Don't rush," Freckles said. "Remember. Walk slow."

"Go."

Freckles nearly tripped on the train of her blue dress.

That's all they needed. Freckles caught her balance and grinned. Suzi inched forward and could see her turn the corner. She couldn't wait to see the men.

"Now me, Mommy?" Kristina asked.

"Just a moment." Bending down, she smoothed the glittering gold dress and her see-through gold veil. "I love you so much. Just think, today you're getting a daddy." Kissing her, she hugged her. Then she heard the music. "Now, baby."

Bouncing, Kristina started out at a run and hauled herself to a halt at the back row. Suzi touched her forehead, breathing a silent sigh of relief. With a grin at her mother, Kristina scooped her hand into the rose petals and tossed them—straight up as high as she could—into the air.

They rained down not only on the aisle in front of them but on people sitting in the pews.

Suzi could hear chuckles. But those chuckles couldn't keep her attention, for her music had just started. Taking a deep breath, she squeezed the red, white, blue and gold carnation bundle in her hands and started out of the side room.

She walked to the end of the aisle where the doors were open and stepped in.

People in sheriffs' uniforms and suits, dresses and nice pants filled the pews. Everyone was there, it seemed. And her family, too. There they stood. At the end of the large church. Julian, Zach and then Mitch. Her daughter was halfway down the aisle, still throwing the petals. Mitch grinned and winked at Kristina, then saw Suzi.

His gaze riveted on her and stayed there.

Everyone stood. Suzi could feel her knees knocking as she started down the aisle.

For the life of her, she couldn't look away from Mitch's gaze. She felt tears brim and slip over her cheeks. She'd never felt joy like this before. Each step brought her closer and closer.

And then she was there. Mitch was holding out his hand and she reached out for it.

"Long walk, Suzi-q?" he whispered, as he pulled her forward next to him.

She smiled softly and, forgetting the audience, she reached up and touched his cheek. "The longest walk of my life."

Covering her hand, he whispered, "You'll never have to walk alone again."

The preacher cleared his throat. "We're here to join this man and this woman—these two friends—" he added.

"Best friends," Suzi whispered.

"—in holy matrimony with God as their leader of this union. May God bless them and keep their hearts close together, united as one, as they are now."

Mitch glanced down as Suzi. "Forever and ever."

"Forever," Suzi mouthed back.

"And Suzi," Mitch whispered, as the pastor started their vows.

"Yes?" she whispered back.

"Looks like you'll be doing my laundry for more than just a month."

The groom's laughter and bride's shriek could be heard a mile away.

Still, there, before all of Hill Creek, Suzi and her best friend joined themselves together in what would become known as one of the best Fourth of July celebrations ever.

* * * * *

Dear Reader,

When I got married, love was such an abstract idea to me. What is love? Does it mean you just fall head over heels and can't look at another person, or is it something I don't really understand? I was certain I loved my husband—but why?

This story, to me, is the basic quality of what love is all about. Friendship. If you aren't friends, nothing else is going to work. After all, friends go out together, talk together, do everything together. You might be great lovers or wonderful parents, but without that friendship, something is missing.

So what happens when best friends realize they are in love? This is a story of tenderness, fun, tragedy and the continuation of some of your favorite characters from the last two stories of HILL CREEK, TEXAS.

Let me know if you're interested in the saga of HILL CREEK, TEXAS, by writing me at P.O. Box 207, Slaughter, LA 70777. Blessings to you all.

In Christ's Love,

Cheryl Wolverton

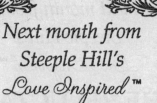

Next month from
Steeple Hill's
Love Inspired™

A FAMILY IN THE MAKING

by

Marcy Froemke

Jilted by her faithless fiancé, Brynn Weston is alone
and in desperate need of a job. She finds the perfect
position—as the nanny for architect Michael Hudson's
daughter. But he thinks she's just trying to catch a
husband. When she sees how much Michael and his
daughter need her help, she's determined to help them
rediscover their faith—in God and in each other.

**Don't miss
A FAMILY IN THE MAKING
On sale July 2000**